~Author Ackn

To John and Ray,
for obvious reasons.

~Available Now / Coming Soon~

Unforgettable

and

Dark Crescendo

Read short previews at the end of this book!

Talk of the Town

Garrett had ached for this moment since he first laid eyes on her. He had to taste her ... feel her ... have her ... now!

Laughing softly, Garrett lowered his face to hers and began nibbling lightly on her ear. "I want you, Samantha," he moaned huskily, "and I can see it in your eyes that you want me—"

Samantha stopped his words by jerking her head to the side. Using all her strength, she tried to writhe free from his iron grasp, but he tightened his hold on her wrist and secured her to the cushions with his weight.

"Let go of me!" she protested, fighting now like a lioness. But his body was on hers like a cement block, pressing harder with each move she made. When she could fight no longer, he released her wrist and urged her face to meet his smoldering gaze.

"It's no use, my love, we can't deny our feelings for each other, so stop fighting it."

There was a wicked glint in his eyes, a warning that he was not a man to be reckoned with. He was used to having his own way. After all, he was a king. He ruled the airwaves late at night, sitting on his leather throne, his crown, a cruel and biting tongue that had the ability to reduce men of power to blubbering fools. What chance did she have against this multi-faceted, self-proclaimed monarch named Tony Garrett?

1

Talk of the Town

by

Lucille Naroian

Licensed and produced by
Penumbra Publishing
www.penumbrapublishing.com

PRINTED IN THE UNITED STATES OF AMERICA
ISBN/EAN-13: 978-1-935563-22-8
Copyright © 2009 Lucille Naroian. All rights reserved.
Cover Photos © Copyright Shutterstock Images LLC. Used with permission.
Also available in Ebook, ISBN/EAN-13: 978-1-935563-08-2

Talk

of the

Town

by

Lucille Narcian

CHAPTER ONE

Tony Garrett walked out under the hot arc lights of Studio 12B to the sound of thunderous applause. The familiar fiery ovation never failed to give him a rush, and he acknowledged the enthusiastic greeting by giving a slight nod of his head, while his eyes quickly scanned the cheering audience. He knew why they were here...what they were expecting ... and he was ready.

The atmosphere continued to crackle with excitement and anticipation as the handsome, controversial, *king* of late night television stopped in center stage and took a deep, long, appreciative bow. It had taken Garrett less than a year to earn the reputation of being the arrogant, hard-hitting, deep-probing, star of the late night news telecast, *One on One*. He had earned it by being unique and ruthless. For it was his direct and incisive style of interviewing that compelled thirty million viewers across the country to tune in faithfully each night at midnight to watch in awe as he interrogated, with utter relentlessness, the guest who sat opposite him in the 'hot seat.'

Whether it was a campaigning politician or a Supreme Court Justice, Garrett showed no mercy. So it was hard to believe that anyone in his right mind would agree to come on his show and subject himself to Garrett's brutal badgering. Strangely enough, they came in droves.

When the members of the audience finally settled themselves comfortably into their seats, Garrett moved towards one of the two easy chairs behind him. He clipped the tiny microphone onto his navy-striped tie, then eased his six-foot-two-inch frame into the soft leather of his seat. Just as he reached for his notes, a short, balding man in shirt sleeves darted out from the side entrance, frantically waving a clipboard. Instinctively, Garrett knew something was wrong.

"Schedule's been changed, Tony!" mumbled the show's producer, Louie Polcheck, as he chewed nervously on his unlit cigar. "Sheffield's a no-show. No word. Nothing."

With fire in his eyes, Garrett glared at the man. "For Chrissake, Louie! What the hell am I supposed to do now? Tap dance for the next sixty minutes? I checked the schedule. You didn't book a back-up just in case. Why not?"

The producer ignored his question, mainly because there was no time for an explanation. He planked his short, stubby hand on his star's taut arm, lowered his head and spoke in a low tone. "Take it easy, will ya? I found a fill-in. Just don't go ballistic on me when you hear what this person does for a living."

The apologetic look on Louie's face gave him away, and Garrett knew by the knot in his gut what Louie was going to say. He tried to control his anger by sucking in a deep, unsteady breath. "I don't give a damn if the guy twirls batons. Just don't tell me it's another one of your Stephen King wannabes."

Louie jerked back his hand and shrugged his round shoulders. "Look, I'm sorry. It was the best I could do under the circumstances. Nobody on the list was immediately available."

Garrett gritted his teeth. "Dammit. Just what I need...another boring flash-in-the-pan hack writer who thinks I'm gonna make him a star." He gave a wry chuckle.

"I'll make him a star all right. By tomorrow morning nobody's going to remember his name, especially me."

He shook his head in irritation while automatically reaching into his breast pocket for his ever-present cigarettes, only to find the pocket empty. Since smoking had been banned in the studio, as in all public buildings, he had decided to quit cold turkey. That had been a month ago. Since then he'd become unbearable to everyone, including himself. God, he needed a smoke, he admitted silently. He'd never get through this night without one.

Eying Louie's unlit cigar with envy, he declared tightly, "You know how I–"

"Put a lid on it!" Louie snapped, tossing his star a sheet of paper. "You got a job to do. Here are the vital stats. Wing it!"

Garrett had no time to argue. The flashing red light on camera three signaling thirty seconds to air time blinked on. With the last chords of his theme song fading away, the camera moved in, and the slow familiar half-smile shaped his lips. In the intimate low voice that was his trademark, Tony Garrett greeted his audience.

"Ladies and gentlemen, last night I announced that our guest tonight would be Paul Sheffield, the sports columnist for The Daily Times. Unfortunately, I've just been informed that the gentleman, and I use the term lightly, is nowhere to be found." The camera zoomed in closer, and Garrett continued sarcastically. "I read his review of last night's fight in this morning's paper, and I'm not surprised he took off. It was a biased, shabby, totally unprofessional piece of work. If I had written it, I'd be hiding, too."

The audience let out a string of boos, but Garrett ignored them. He raised a dark eyebrow in distaste, then

3

lowered his eyes to the paper. "Lucky for us, my crack staff has come up with a sleeper. Ever heard of Sam McCall?" he asked rhetorically. "Well, neither have I. But we're all stuck with him for the next fifty-six minutes." He raised his cool blue eyes to the camera. "According to this note, McCall has just published his first whodunit. Sorry, but I don't have a copy here to show you. Anyway, the book is entitled, *Murder in Paradise,* and after this short break we'll be right back to find out who did it." The words were practically stuck in his throat. "I can hardly wait. Can you?" He averted his gaze from the camera to the studio audience then back to the camera again, shrugging his broad shoulders. "On the other hand, who cares?" he mocked indifferently. "It's probably a drugged-out chimp with a bag of loaded coconuts."

A conspiratorial wink at the audience was the last the home viewers saw before a three minute string of commercials flashed on their screens.

* * * * *

Behind the green satin curtain, Sam McCall seethed. "Who in the hell does this clown think he is?" the author sputtered to no one in particular. For the last five minutes the young writer had been witness to a despicable show of manners, been ridiculed, and made a national joke. "All right, Big Mouth," the writer enunciated on a hiss, "you got your shots in. Now, it's my turn." Adrenaline pumping wildly, the writer began pacing behind the curtain like a caged animal until finally, it was show time.

Garrett was straightening his tie when the camera light blinked on. Without bothering to look towards the curtain,

4

he unenthusiastically announced, "Ladies and gentlemen, Mr. Sam McCall."

In place of the usual polite applause afforded an unknown, the audience set up a howl of laughter. Perplexed, Garrett shifted in his seat as a wisp of a girl emerged from the shadows. He rose to his feet, and his athletic frame towered above the five-foot-nothing loveliness that was Sam McCall. Completely taken aback, Garrett gave an appreciative smile to the petite, auburn-haired girl. He automatically extended his large tanned hand and offered, "This is indeed a pleasant surprise."

Ignoring his outstretched hand, she looked directly into his startled gaze and ever so sweetly replied, "I'm glad you feel that way, Mr. Garrett, because I've got another one for you." Without a warning, she raised her right hand and smashed her fragile fingers into the side of his powerful jaw. Feeling exuberant, she turned on her heels, squared her shoulders, and strutted off the stage.

Momentarily stunned, the audience did not react. And then, as if on cue, row after row came to its feet in a burst of deafening applause.

Totally unaware of the havoc she had created with her impetuous show of temperament, Samantha snatched up her coat and purse and fled through the double doors that led to a bank of elevators. Angrily pressing the down button with her still tingling fingers, she was struck suddenly by the full realization of what she had just done. Like a frightened rabbit, she dashed into the elevator as soon as the doors parted. Once outside the mammoth complex, Samantha ran to the nearest taxi. Wrenching the door open, she nearly stumbled in her haste to escape. In a calm voice that belied her quaking state, she gave the driver the name of her hotel.

Immediately, the taxi veered into the flowing traffic.

Her breathing began to come in spasms, so she wedged her trembling body against the door in an effort to calm herself. Unfortunately, the harder she tried, the more anxious she became. She buried her face in her hands and began berating herself out loud, completely ignoring the driver and the fact that he could hear every word.

"Mother of God, Samantha," she groaned, "You've done some pretty outrageous things in your life, but you've never pulled a classic like this, and on television, yet. Tomorrow morning it'll be splashed across every newspaper in the country. Regis and Kelly will have a good howl for themselves along with the girls on *The View*. There goes your career right down the toilet before it even got off the ground." She flicked away an angry tear that threatened to spill. "Why did you have to make a spectacle of yourself by hitting him? You're not an irrational person. Better you had just split, leaving him sitting on his royal throne with egg on his face. But no, not you. You had to play the avenging angel out to slay the evil dragon. Well, be prepared for this evil dragon to strike back." Panic rose within her and she muttered out loud, "'Cause now he's gonna get you!"

"Who's gonna get me, lady?" the driver asked nervously.

Flaming with embarrassment, Samantha was saved an explanation as the cab came to a halt before the lighted entrance to the hotel. She quickly passed the driver a twenty dollar bill and bolted from the taxi without waiting for her change.

Once inside the ornate lobby she approached the desk clerk and asked for her key. The man gave her an odd smile as he handed it to her. Snatching the key from his scrawny fingers, she noticed a tiny television set next to his computer. So *that* was the reason for his dumb grin, she reasoned. He had seen the show. The nightmare was beginning all ready.

Once inside her room, she dropped to the edge of her bed. Her heart pounded like a marathon runner, but she was safe, at least for the time being. Maybe if she crawled under the bed covers and went to sleep, she would wake in the morning to find it had just been a horrible dream. Maybe...

The ringing of the telephone on the night stand beside her brought Samantha out of her musings. Who could be calling, she wondered, her heart skipping a beat. Perhaps it was a member of Garrett's staff informing her of a law suit. On the chance her instincts were on target, she decided not to answer it. She needed time to think ... to finagle a way out of this mess.

Under ordinary circumstances, that wouldn't have been such a monumental task, if she weren't so exhausted. After all, extricating oneself from sticky situations was her stock-in-trade. Her characters were pros at it. But at this moment, all she could do was simply grab her camel-haired jacket and toss it over a nearby chair.

She was just about to kick off her shoes when she was startled by a frantic pounding on the door. "What now?" she cried in a strangled voice.

Before she could decide whether or not to answer it, the door flew open, and a short, bespectacled man rushed in flailing an angry fist in the air. Feeling she was about to incur the same fate as Tony Garrett, she quickly shielded her face by crossing both arms in front of it.

"Don't worry," the man snarled, "I'm not going to hit you, even though the urge to do it is overwhelming!"

Samantha lowered her arms. "You saw it, didn't you," she said anxiously.

"The whole bloody world saw it, *Rocky*!" he bellowed, turning from her in a huff. Then he whirled back around and faced her again, his dark eyes blazing behind round silver-framed glasses. "Whatever possessed you to do it?"

"He insulted me!" she exclaimed, exasperated.

"So you whacked him? Knowing you were on live television?" he roared. "Don't you know how powerful this guy really is? He can make or break you with a phone call. And my guess is that by tomorrow morning, you'll be on a plane back to Florida."

Samantha became indignant. "Now just one minute, Adam. I'm the injured party here, not that pompous ass who thinks he's God's gift to the media! Truth is, he's the host from Hell, and I'll bet my laptop there isn't a viewer who doesn't agree with me!" Her tawny green eyes narrowed with her fury and she began to march toward him.

The short, slightly-built man extended his palms out as if to hold her at bay while hastening backwards, matching her quick-paced steps, only to be halted by the cedar wood door behind him.

The color that now stained her cheeks matched her long auburn tresses, and her small sensuous mouth tightened, accentuating her gorgeous dimples.

Adam Pearce braced himself for the explosion, and it came with full force. "Just before air time, that peacock had the unmitigated gall to refer to me as a flash-in-the-pan, boring *hack* writer whom no one would remember tomorrow morning! Well, after tonight I doubt that the name Sam McCall will be so easily forgotten. In fact, it will probably become a household word!"

"I don't doubt it," Adam returned, clamping both his hands on her upper arms. "But it would be for the wrong reason."

"I can't help that now," she retorted regretfully. "What's done is done and can't be changed." She pulled herself free, then walked back to the bed, her fury spent. "Look," she said, sighing as she glanced at the clock on her night stand, "it's late and I'm beat. I don't want to talk about this incident anymore, so let's just call it a night."

Adam Pearce backed off, but only for a moment. "We have to talk about it, Samantha." His tone was stern. "This *incident* is not a closed matter. Not by a long shot." He pushed his hand deep into his jacket pocket, removed a wrinkled slip of paper, and tossed it to her. "That's Garrett's private number at the studio. He's still there. I suggest–"

"Where did you get this?" she asked, staring at the number.

Adam cleared his throat. He knew he was in for round two. "From Garrett himself."

Her eyes widened with disbelief. "You actually went to the studio to see him?"

"I had to do something to save your butt!" he practically screeched. "The guy was fit to kill. You should have seen his face. It was the color of a frozen veal chop. Now, give him a call and apologize, because if you don't, then you can kiss your career goodbye."

For a moment, Samantha considered Adam's demand, then crumpled the paper into a ball and tossed it back to him. "You know what you can do with this."

Adam gave her a hard look. "You're making a big mistake if you don't play ball with this guy. He's not a man to be reckoned with ... if you get my drift."

9

His *drift* was disgustingly clear. But Samantha was her own person who didn't crumble under threats of any kind. "I hear you," she said, trying to keep her voice light. "But I'm *not* going to call him, and that's *my* final answer! Now go! I still have things to do. I'm scheduled to be at Barnes and Noble tomorrow morning at eleven for a book signing session, or have you forgotten?"

"Hardly," he said, forcing a smile. "That's the reason why you're here."

Samantha suffered a moment of apprehension. "You will be there, won't you?"

"*Rocky,*" I wouldn't miss this for the world."

He was about to close the door behind him when he stopped and said curtly, "Keep this door locked! This is New York City, not Home Sweet Home."

As soon as he left, she locked the door, removed her clothes, then tossed them on the chair beside the television. Deciding on a quick shower in place of a hot bath, after which she slipped into her flannel nightgown, she gave a long stretch and a yawn, then crawled beneath the warm covers, thoroughly exhausted. She had expected sleep to come instantly, but her mind kept racing back over the events of the day ... events that would leave indelible marks on her memory forever.

* * * * *

She had arrived in New York City late that afternoon after a smooth flight from Tampa, Florida, the sun-bathed city where she and her parents vacationed every winter. Her purpose in coming was to promote the sale of her novel, *Murder in Paradise*. Not a story for the squeamish, the book boasted a plot rich in violence and gore – a guaranteed page-turner for those with a strong stomach. Surprisingly enough, the book was not Samantha's first, as Garrett had so rudely pointed out, but was her third. And although the previous two had been published, they literally went nowhere. It was her new agent, Adam Pearce, who had spotted what *he* considered might be the problem.

"I know there are lots of women who are writing some great mysteries," he had said over the telephone one gray and rainy morning. "But if I were in the market for a spine-tingler where the killer was a psycho with an ax collection, I wouldn't reach for a book written by a girl named Samantha. The name is too soft, too–"

"That's a sexist thing to say, especially in this day and age!" she had blurted out before he had a chance to finish.

"I knew you'd feel that way, and you're right. It is. But I'm in the business of selling books to one of the biggest publishers in New York. The point to remember is that your genre is hard-core murder mysteries, and by using your given name, I feel you've put yourself at a disadvantage. To give you a perfectly good example, I personally know two guys that write romance novels that would curl your toes. After I talked to them they realized that romance junkies would never accept the fact that two men named Leon and Nunzio could relate to the way a woman thinks and feels, so they write under female pseudonyms and everybody's happy. Then along comes this Waller guy who writes a soul-wrenching tear-jerker called *The Bridges of Madison County* under his own name and shoots the hell out of that theory. Go figure. All I know is that from where I sit, he's the exception, not the rule."

Samantha was becoming bored with his ramblings. It

was time to make her point. "Agatha Christie made it, along with Mary Higgins Clark and countless others, and they all used their own names."

"Correct," he had agreed. "But again, your stories aren't the run of the mill whodunits, they're ... they're..." He struggled for the right word and found it. "Macabre. But don't listen to me. You just keep your killers hacking away, and some day, if you're lucky–"

"All right, Adam, I give up. What do you suggest?" she had asked with a sigh, mentally visualizing herself living in a cold-water flat, collecting Social Security checks, while pounding away on her computer, determined to achieve recognition before the wretched Angel of Death rapped on her door shouting, "Enough all ready!"

Laughter punctuated Adam's reply. "It's so simple! Just shorten Samantha to Sam!"

When she had failed to respond immediately to his suggestion, he jumped back in. "Yes. That's it. Sam McCall. I like it. Don't you?"

Samantha finally found her voice. "No, I don't. People will think I'm a man. But you're the expert, so I'd better agree."

In the months following that conversation, Samantha penned several short stories using her new name. To her amazement, they had all been accepted by detective magazines. That little taste of success was like an aphrodisiac. Soon, Samantha decided to try the novel route once again. She submitted *Murder in Paradise* to her present publisher, and within six months the book had shown promise ... real promise. Adam Pearce had been right.

On this particular morning, Samantha was relaxing

over coffee when Adam called. Samantha could barely decipher his words with all the excitement in his voice. "Pack a suitcase and catch the first flight out to New York City. I've just spoken to your publisher and he's arranged book signing sessions at several of the major book stores. He's even managed a guest appearance on *Good Morning America* the day after tomorrow."

"But–"

"No buts about it, young lady." His voice was stern and uncompromising. "You need all the publicity you can get."

Samantha's heart began pounding rapidly, and her knees went weak. "But Adam, I've never been to New York City. I wouldn't know my way around. And except for a one-liner in my high school play, I've never spoken before a group of people. I'd freeze at the sight of a television camera."

"Not to worry," he had assured her. "I've booked a room for you at the Sheraton New York. When you get off the plane, take a taxi to 7th Avenue and 52nd Street. Call me as soon as you get in." Without waiting for an answer, he had said goodbye and hung up. There had been no chance for a rebuttal, no chance to voice the suffusion of doubt and apprehension that had taken hold of her.

She was still gripping the receiver when her father entered the study. Upon hearing the light tapping of his cane on the polished hardwood floor, she turned and raised anxious eyes to meet his puzzled stare. "Trouble?" he had asked with parental concern.

"Just the opposite, Dad," she had replied, placing the receiver back on its cradle. "That was my agent. He wants me to go to New York immediately for a promotional tour for my book."

"So why the frown?" he had asked, slowly lowering his arthritic-frame into the seat beside her. "This is the day you've been dreaming about. Your mother and I are so proud of you."

Samantha's eyes brimmed with tears. "I love you both for having so much faith in me. I don't ever want to be a disappointment to you." She paused and took a deep breath. It's just ... for some unexplained reason, I'm scared."

Jerome McCall had laughed heartily. "You? Scared? You've never been afraid of anything in your life." He raised the cane slightly and tapped it against her shoe. "Now go and pack some warm clothes. I'll call the airport. I have a few connections there. Maybe I can get one of them to pull a string or two and get you on the next flight out to New York."

Upstairs in her room, Samantha had packed the warmest outfits she had, remembering as she closed the lid to include the notes for her new book. Due to be on her publisher's desk on January second, the book was not yet completed, leaving only three weeks to reach the deadline. She made a mental note of the date as she pushed her laptop computer into the suitcase, grabbed her purse, then hurried down the stairs and into the car where her parents were waiting.

She didn't have long to wait at the airport. As soon as her flight was called, Samantha threw her arms around the beaming couple. "Wish me luck," she had said, smothering them with kisses. After her mother had given her one last embrace, her father cupped her chin. "Opportunity is knocking, honey. Now get on that plane and when you get to New York I want you to knock 'em dead."

* * * * *

Knock them dead? She groaned into her pillow, remembering the startled gaze on Tony Garrett's face. Good God, she had almost knocked him out!

Recalling that impetuous act, Samantha bolted upright in her bed. Suppose her father had seen the broadcast and it was *he* who had telephoned earlier to express his shame and disappointment in her. That was a distinct possibility. On the other hand, it was most unlikely. She was to be a fill-in, so her appearance on the show had not been publicized. Not only that, the show was a live telecast and not taped at an earlier time like the rest of the talk shows. She sighed in relief. He couldn't have been the caller. It must have been Adam.

Samantha dropped her aching head back onto the pillow and relived, in full detail, the moments that had led up to that disastrous encounter with Tony Garrett.

* * * * *

As soon as she had checked into the hotel and unpacked her suitcase, she had called Adam as he had instructed. It seemed only moments had passed before he was rapping enthusiastically on her door. His greeting had been warm and exciting.

"Welcome to the Big Apple!" he had exclaimed, and as though he were welcoming royalty, he placed a dozen American Beauty roses in her arms. She breathed in their sweet, delicate aroma. "Is this how you treat all your clients?"

15

"No," he drawled, "just the redheaded *girls* named Sam. I've never given flowers to a man. Although, I remember the time a guy sent me a potted palm with an invitation to a dinner dance."

Samantha couldn't tell if he was serious or not. "What did you do?"

"I went, silly," he said, grinning like an elf. "A man has to eat. But I refused to dance with him. I do have my standards."

Samantha giggled. "You're putting me on."

"About the dinner dance, yes. The plant, no. Some writers will do anything to get published. Little do they realize that I only present their manuscripts to publishers. I guarantee nothing."

He clasped his hands together. "You must be starved. How about dinner? It's on me."

After a delightful afternoon of stimulating conversation, sumptuous food, and several glasses of the smoothest French wine she had ever tasted, Samantha was deposited at the front door of her hotel by an apologetic Adam. Explaining his need to attend a meeting, Adam had assured Samantha that he would be with her in the morning to lend her moral support.

After taking a long, relaxing bubble bath, she had just settled down to work on her manuscript when the telephone rang. It was Adam, and he was exuberant. "You'll never believe the break you're about to get!" he exclaimed. "You, lucky girl, are going to be the only guest tonight on the Tony Garrett show."

Samantha went cold. "Oh, no I'm not!" she protested vehemently. "I've never seen him but I've heard about him. He's got a wicked reputation for being brutal to his guests.

He'd make minced meat out of me."

There was a moment of silence, then Adam declared, "One look at you and he'll be eating out of your hands. Now put your glad rags on and get over to the studio as fast as you can!" After giving her the address, he reassured her that although he couldn't be there, all would go well. She was a pro. He had complete faith in her.

Ironically, his parting comment had been the same as her father's. *Knock 'em dead.*

CHAPTER TWO

At 7:00 a.m. Samantha decided that she and her bed should part company. She had barely slept a wink, and now, sitting on the side of the bed, she felt the stab of a nagging headache behind her temples. Luckily she had remembered to bring some aspirin. Stifling a yawn, she padded wearily to the bathroom for water. What she really needed was coffee, strong and hot, to not only clear the cobwebs from her brain, but according to the brightly-lit mirror above the sink, to also open her blurry eyes which stared back at her at half-mast.

No sooner had she dialed for room service and returned to the bathroom to brush her teeth, when an energetic knock at the door released an agitated grumble from her lips. "It couldn't possibly be him," she mumbled on her way to the door. When she opened it, she made a desperate attempt at calm as her eyes brought into focus the excited figure of a man garbed in a bright red jogging suit, grinning back at her from behind a cloth-covered cart.

"Your coffee, *Rocky*," Adam Pearce drawled as he pushed the cart past her into the room.

"What are you doing here at this hour?" Samantha asked impatiently. "Don't you have a home?"

"Of course," he replied, giving her a sly little wink. "But I couldn't start the day without first checking in on the champ. And might I add that you're looking mighty nifty this morning."

Samantha rolled her eyes heavenward, then stepped around to the cart and scoffed, "Moonlighting for the hotel on the side, Adam?"

"No, silly. I was on my way up here when I met the busboy in the hall. So I slipped him a dime and he let me take the cart. Money talks, Samantha."

Exasperated, Samantha shook her head and poured herself some coffee. With cup in hand, she sat down on the chair in front of the desk. Looking like the cat who swallowed the canary, Adam walked over to her and unzipped his jacket, from which he extracted the morning edition of the *New York Daily News*. "Well, girl," he said, waving the paper before her, "you're a full fledged celebrity now. You made the front page of the *News*."

Samantha almost choked on her coffee. "Let me see that!" She snatched the tabloid from his hand. Her eyes narrowed in disgust as they focused on the photograph of herself and Tony Garrett taken the split second her hand had struck his jaw. "This is terrible!" she gasped, unable to subdue her anger.

"Your publisher happens to agree," he admitted. "In fact, he called me at six this morning, fit to be tied."

Samantha didn't take that news well at all. "Why is *he* upset? None of this reflects on him."

Adam perched himself on the edge of the desk. "Well, it does and it doesn't. What happened can't touch the publishing company. That's a given. What's upsetting Bob is that he was at the television studio last night, for whatever reason, and he overheard someone say that Garrett's guest didn't show up. So Bob told a member of the staff that he could come up with a replacement. That's where you and I come in. Bob knew you were in town, so he called me to get you on the show. He figured Garrett might go easy on you and ruffle your feathers just a bit. He never figured you'd

19

belt the guy. Now he feels you owe Garrett an apology–"

"Stop right there!" she said roughly. She was tired of all this, and she wasn't going to take any more. "Get this through your thick head, buddy, I'm *not* going to apologize to him! End of subject!"

Adam placed his hands on his hips. "Why are you being so adamant about this?"

"Because I refuse to apologize to anyone who verbally attacks and intimidates me and my craft. So he hates mystery writers. Tough! Not only that, it's *his* personal opinion so he should have kept it to himself. Some pro. For God's sake, Adam, he was so unprepared he didn't even know I was a woman! If he had kept his big mouth shut before introducing me, I would have gone on. I'm aware of his reputation. I told you that. And I *know* I could have held my own. *Then* if he began his badgering act, I simply would've just gotten up and left, and none of this would have happened. But it didn't work out that way. So, if he's going to sue me for assaulting him, what can I do? Question now is, do you think he'll take action against me?"

Adam replied with confidence. "I doubt it. He wouldn't dare. He knows he screwed up. Personally, I feel that *he* should apologize to you!"

"Agreed," she said with a wide smile.

Adam pointed to the article. "You might feel better if you read this. You've got the public on your side. More importantly, you've won over the press. They loved it. You're the talk of the town. That little love tap you laid on Garrett did more for your book than a nationwide tour." He hopped off the desk. "Gotta run," he said, heading for the door. "Gotta get my two blocks in before the muggers wake up and hit the streets. Enjoy your coffee. I'll see you later at the book store."

As soon as Adam left, Samantha went back to the desk and picked up the newspaper. Her gaze focused intently on the damning photograph. With a sinking heart, her eyes blotted out her image so that all she could see was Tony Garrett's startled profile.

Last night she had looked at him for no more than a minute or two. Yet, somehow his magnetic presence had taken command of not only his audience, but of her as well. Worse yet, the more he continued to malign her, the more his handsome face and tall, broad frame branded itself in her brain. It wasn't until now that she realized the impact he had made upon her.

As she stood there listening to him tear her and her book apart, the writer inside her had raged at his insensitivity, and it was this part of her personality that had dominated and acted on impulse. But it was the feminine part of her that had registered his manliness. Now that she could finally assimilate her thoughts, she remembered how his cool blue eyes had mirrored his pleasure when she appeared before him.

"What he must think of me," she murmured softly, momentarily blotting out everything that had happened. At this moment, the balancing scales of who was right and who was wrong seemed to fizzle itself out. "Right now he's probably wishing I'd crawl under some rock, and he's right. If I had any sense at all, I'd go back to Tampa and put all this behind me, because if I stay here in New York, I'll never live it down." Then she remembered her publisher, and of course Adam, both of whom were paramount to her career. She couldn't let them down. Not only them, there were her folks to consider. Panic gripped her a second time.

If the picture appeared in the Tampa newspapers, her family would be subjected to a rainfall of flippant remarks and merciless ridicule, heaping upon them unnecessary shame and embarrassment, and all because in a momentary burst of temperament, she had managed to attract nationwide attention.

Becoming more depressed by the minute, Samantha shook her head to rid herself of the distressing thoughts, then dropped the newspaper back down on the desk. She couldn't afford to think of anything now but the book signing session ahead. Later, when she returned to the hotel, she'd call Bob and her folks and explain everything.

An hour later, Samantha smiled confidently at her reflection in the mirror hanging above the colonial-styled bureau. She had taken a long invigorating shower and slipped into a deep green pants suit with a white cowl neck sweater. Her lustrous red hair swung loose and full around her shoulders. As for her makeup, a touch of mascara along with a dab of colorless gloss on her pink lips completed her grooming. She looked absolutely radiant as she gathered up her jacket and brown leather purse and headed for the elevator door at exactly ten thirty.

Once outside the hotel, Samantha became immediately enthralled with the magical metropolis. Sky- scrapers crammed together as high and as far as the eye could see, were in direct contrast to the palm-tree-lined streets of Tampa. Immediately caught up in the hustle and bustle around her, she wished she had allowed herself extra time to tour the city and shop. Christmas was only two weeks away, and the windows of the more elegant stores like Saks and Lord & Taylor were certain to be dressed in spectacular holiday adornment. But she feared being late for her appointment with Adam, so stepping to the curb, she waved down an approaching taxi. Within minutes she pushed open the door to Barnes & Noble.

The bookstore was mobbed. Ardent readers huddled in corners and around book-covered tables, their arms laden with their purchases. Samantha anxiously scanned the crowd and saw to her relief, Adam Pearce busily stacking her books in neat piles on a bridge table at the far end of the checkout counter.

"Adam!" she called out, weaving her way through the mob. At the sound of his name, Adam looked up and opened his arms to greet her with a smile and a friendly hug. "What do you think of this?" he asked, pointing to a cardboard display of her. Beneath the glossy cutout were stacks of white-jacketed, hard-covered volumes of *Murder in Paradise.*

"Oh, Adam, I love it!" she squealed in delight.

"So do they," he said, pointing to the crowd that was beginning to circle the table. "The book is a smash already. "I'll lay odds that by the time you leave here, the display and table will be empty. Now, step around over here, my dear, and watch the magic happen."

Samantha removed her jacket and placed it over the back of a folding chair. Adam clapped his hands and raised his voice loudly enough to be heard above the chattering crowd. "Ladies and gentlemen, may I have your attention, please. This is the moment you've been waiting for. And now it gives me great pleasure to present the star of the day, Miss Sam McCall."

Whistles and cheers followed Adam's brief presentation, and immediately, Samantha was bombarded by autograph-seekers who pushed and shoved each other in their quest to obtain her signature. Ecstatic by their propellant response, Samantha penned her name on each book as fast as she could, inwardly amazed at the number of people who shared her fancy for the macabre. What made it more amazing was the fact that her pursuers were mostly female, and she couldn't resist the urge to mention it to one young lady who was practically breathless as she planked her book into Samantha's hands.

"I'm delighted to know you share my passion for thrillers," Samantha said coolly, attempting to sound extremely professional.

"Oh, I don't read these things," the girl replied offhandedly. "I just want your autograph. And I wasn't sure you'd give it to me unless I bought your book. You're the girl who slapped Tony Garrett's face last night on television. I just loooooooove Tony Garrett. He's so handsome and sexy, and I know this is the closest I'll ever get to him." The girl then brazenly took Samantha's right hand and clasped it in hers. "Ooooooh," she squealed, practically soaring off into orbit. "I just held the hand that touched Tony Garrett!"

The blood in Samantha's veins ran cold. So *he* was the reason for all this activity. It had nothing to do with her book. It was merely the vehicle by which she was being exploited. Adam had been right. She was famous now, but for the wrong reason. Angered to the bone, she turned around to find Adam staring off into space. The fixed grin on his lips and the faraway look in his eyes assured Samantha that he was mentally tabulating the book sales and calculating his share of the profits. Grasping him by the coat sleeve, Samantha mumbled through clenched teeth, "I'm leaving this place right now. These people aren't interested in my book. They only want a souvenir of last night's fiasco."

Adam quickly returned to earth. "You're not going anywhere!" he snapped. "These people are shelling out good money for your book, and you're going to sign every one. Why do you care why they're buying it? The point is, they're buying it. Stay focused. When the book soars to number one on the New York Times best seller list, it won't put the reason why in parenthesis beside it. What it *will* do is almost guarantee the success of your next one. Understand how it works now?"

He didn't wait for an answer, but took her hand and pulled her aside so that she could see out the entrance doors. "Look," he said harshly, "the line goes all the way down the street. Those people want your autograph, and they're willing to buy the book to get it. That's precisely why you're here. Now get back to the table and give them what they want. When it's over, we'll grab a bite to eat and you can vent your grievances to your heart's content. Now get!"

Samantha obeyed, all the while feeling absolutely sick inside. She signed book after book and listened half-heatedly to the favorable comments about her performance on the program the previous night. Not once was she criticized for what she had done. In fact, she was considered a heroine – a symbol of courage, who had taken a stand in defense against one man's biased opinion. In part, it was an outpouring of positive support on her behalf, and it should have been victorious. But somehow, it only made her feel miserable.

Halfway through the session, Samantha once again heard the crowd raise its voice in energetic cheer. Inquisitively, she lifted her gaze and saw two young men slice their way through the mob and proceed toward her.

One man held a cordless microphone while the other supported a portable television camera on his shoulder. Realizing why they were here, she instinctively wanted to escape, but Adam quickly joined her at the table and pinned her hand to her thigh with his while flashing that cat-like grin she was fast becoming acquainted with.

As soon as the reporter reached Samantha, he smiled politely and introduced himself. "How do you do, Miss McCall? My name is Eliot Simpson. I'm with Station WINZ, and I'm here to do a short interview that will be aired on the six and eleven o'clock news tonight." He was perceptive enough to see she was camera-shy, for she blushed profusely, and her entire body stiffened as the camera man approached. Tapping her lightly on the shoulder, the reporter said warmly, "Relax. This isn't going to hurt a bit. It might help if you keep your eyes focused on me. It'll be just like talking to a friend."

Samantha's angry gaze swept to Adam, which was returned with a cold stare. Although she couldn't prove it, she had a gut feeling he was a party to this added humiliation. She longed to accuse him outright despite the crowd, but she didn't utter a word. She was trapped like a spider caught in a web with no alternative but to go along with the interview.

The cameraman gave Eliot Simpson a signal. Fuming inwardly, Samantha boldly decided to set their heads spinning.

The red light atop the camera blinked on and the reporter turned in its direction. "This is Eliot Simpson reporting from Barnes & Noble on Fifth Avenue in New York City. As you can see, an impressive crowd has gathered here to meet a young lady who has taken the city by storm. Her name is Sam McCall, and she's here to promote her book, *Murder in Paradise* which, by all indications here, is destined to become a best seller." He looked away from the camera to meet Samantha's solemn face. "Welcome to New York City, Miss McCall."

"Thank you," she answered, her voice chillingly cold.

"How do you feel about all this?" he queried, gesturing toward the heavy throng around them.

Looking squarely into the camera, Samantha took a deep breath then said, "If I had written a book to inform or better mankind, I would feel excited and most appreciative. Unfortunately, that's not the reason for this commotion today." Just as she had anticipated, Samantha's straightforwardness had caught Eliot Simpson off guard, for he began to laugh nervously. "Are you implying your book *isn't* the reason for your notoriety?"

"I'm not implying anything, Mr. Simpson," she replied, her expression hard and unrelenting. "I'm stating a fact."

"Which is?"

Her eyes took on an ominous gleam. "I just told you. My book has nothing to do with this mob scene. It has everything to do with my appearance on the Tony Garrett Show last night. These people came here to see me in person and to congratulate me for having, shall we say, chutzpah?"

Eliot Simpson's face remained expressionless as he picked up a book from the table and examined it carefully. "Must they express their congratulations by purchasing a book?" he asked, almost sarcastically.

Samantha interpreted that question as a low blow and replied accordingly. "Of course not. I'd be happy to give my autograph to anyone who wants it, whether it's in a book or a slip of paper. But I know what you're implying, so let's get to it. Had I not slapped the face of the gentleman, and I use the term loosely, I would still be here. This was a prescheduled promotion for my book."

The reporter went on. "Do you feel you were justified in doing what you did?"

"Absolutely," she said, feeling now the same stirrings of anger she had experienced the previous night. "Regardless of any personal opinions Tony Garrett might have towards writers ... er ... hack writers, as he calls us, he had no cause to insult me or my craft. His status in the media gives him no license to be rude or insolent, at least not where I'm concerned."

Eliot Simpson hesitated a moment, and Samantha noticed a slight smile form on his thin lips. "Would you agree to appear on his show again?" he asked enthusiastically.

Samantha didn't hesitate to answer. "Certainly. But I wouldn't do so without a public apology first." She stifled the urge to laugh. "But the chance of that happening, I'm sure, is very unlikely."

Smiling broadly now, the reporter nodded to the camera. "Well, ladies and gentlemen, Tony Garrett has just been challenged to a return match by this courageous young lady. Will he accept, or will he decline? This is Eliot Simpson for Station WINZ." The red light on the camera blinked off, and Samantha turned to face the reporter. "I hope you got what you came for." she said with cool disdain. "I'd hate to have disappointed you."

Eliot Simpson extended his hand to her. "On the contrary, you were terrific, absolutely terrific. It was a pleasure meeting you, Miss McCall. Good luck with your book." With that, he joined the cameraman, and the two disappeared into the crowd.

* * * * *

Tony Garrett watched the men leave the book store with a grin on his face. He was garbed in a gray overcoat with the collar turned up, and a matching soft hat whose brim touched the rim of his Foster Grants. A fake mustache topped off his disguise, which allowed him to maneuver about the store totally unnoticed. Clutched to his chest were four newspapers and an autographed copy of *Murder in Paradise*.

Just before the interview, he had wedged himself in the midst of the squealing mob of customers who were almost combative in their quest to be next in line. He had set the book before her, hoping she would look up at him and ask his name so that she could personalize the autograph. But she hadn't. Surprisingly, a pang of disappointment had caught him off guard. He had wanted her to look at him ... wanted her to smile at him, even if it meant nothing more than a show of appreciation for braving the barrage of females. But she was angry, just as she was the night before – angry to learn that the only reason the crowd had come was to touch the hand that had slapped his face. He knew that the autograph-seeker's admission as to why she was there had cut Samantha to the quick, and for the first time in his career, Garrett felt shame and remorse. She hadn't deserved his insolent remarks.

Seating himself down on a nearby easy chair that allowed him full view of her, he suddenly felt a mixture of self-hate and frustration slowly begin to build deep within him, for he was all too aware that arrogance and sarcasm were not only despicable traits to possess, but were inexcusable to hurl around at will. Yet he did it, night after night. And it paid off big time. His ratings attested to it. His audience ate it up. They couldn't get enough of the ... *king*.

Gazing forlornly at the beauty who sat at the table at the front of the store, Garrett didn't feel like a king; he felt like a heel.

Last night, as soon as the show was over, he had called her hotel room to apologize. While dialing, he sent up a silent prayer that she would answer. He was willing to put his pride in his pocket and explain that being arrogant and intimidating was what he *did* and not who he *was*, and could she ever forgive him. But she didn't answer the phone. Disappointed to say the least, he had just hung up when Adam Pearce had knocked on his dressing room door. He had come to apologize for Samantha, to explain about her impetuousness, and ask if was there anything *he* could do to amend things. Somehow Pearce's attempt at playing mediator had enraged Garrett. He didn't want to talk to her agent, he wanted to talk to *her*. So he jotted his private number down on a piece of paper and flung it at the man. Pearce sheepishly apologized for his intrusion, and was out the door in a flash.

Garrett had waited in his dressing room until three in the morning for the phone call that never came. Unaccustomed to being disappointed in both his career and personal life, he had no choice but to admit defeat. He picked up his coat and went home.

Two hours later he had consumed half a bottle of Jack Daniels, suffered through reruns of Gilligan's Island and My

Three Sons, and still he couldn't sleep. Lying awake in the darkness, he couldn't forget the fire in her smoldering green eyes, branded in his mind along with the way her dimples deepened as she thrust her head back just before she struck him. Funny, but in that brief, explosive moment, he still was able to take in her navy blue suit with the skirt a good three inches above her knees. Although she had short legs, they were fabulous legs – legs he had ached to feel wrapped around his thighs, pinning him deep inside her. Unfortunately, there wasn't enough Jack Daniels in the world that could enable him to blot out his fantasy last night. It had left him with an arousal so strong, it hurt. Even now, as he watched her signing away, oblivious to his presence, it still hurt.

She was a fighter, in every sense of the word. And what little he'd seen of her in action, he loved. She was different ... earthly ... one of a kind. Not like the starlets who clung to him, hoping to have their names linked romantically with his. Sure, he had been attracted to them, but that's as far as it went. Not one had ever captivated him like this.

Samantha jumped up from her seat, bringing Garrett out of his thoughts. She was arguing with Adam while reaching for her jacket. Garrett glanced at his wristwatch and noted the time. He had a luncheon meeting in less than an hour.

By the time he got to the checkout counter and paid for his papers and book, Samantha and Adam were gone.

CHAPTER THREE

Samantha couldn't get away from the bookstore fast enough. Keeping her eyes focused straight ahead, she marched along the street, refusing to look at her companion.

Adam couldn't stand the strained silence any longer. If ever he needed his sense of humor to break the tension, he needed it now. He decided to make a corny remark. He knew she was devastated. He couldn't blame her.

"I know why you're acting like a witch," he announced, flashing his silly grin. "You're having a PMS attack, right?"

Samantha shot him a baleful look and refrained from commenting. She was reiterating in her mind the conversation she'd just engaged in with Eliot Simpson, and the fact it would be aired on the news that night. Her heart sank. This time her family would see it. They definitely would call. What would she say? What *could* she say?

When Samantha didn't answer, Adam tried again. "I'll bet you're as hungry as a horse. What say we eat? I'm starved, too. We've got a long day ahead of us."

"I'm drained," she admitted, slowing down her pace.

"I can understand that," he replied. "It was quite a session. But you can't let it get the better of you. Did you really think no one was going to mention last night?"

"No," she said, honestly. "It's just that I feel like a failure. Let's face it, if I hadn't made a spectacle of myself on the show last night, the store probably would've been empty." She stopped in her tracks and grabbed at Adam's coat sleeve. "How many men would you say bought my book?"

Adam was trapped, but he had to be honest with her. "I'd say about a dozen."

"A dozen," she repeated. "That's what I figured."

"But you sold two hundred!" he exclaimed. "So let's not go over this again. As far as I'm concerned, you made a killing. Pardon the pun. Now let's decide where we're going to eat. We can stay on this street or go two blocks down. There's a great Italian restaurant that serves spaghetti with the best calamari sauce you've ever tasted. We can have a little vino, then top it off with a hot cappuccino."

Samantha wrinkled her nose. "You're forgetting I'm Irish. What's calamari?"

Adam shot her a strange look. "Don't they have Italian restaurants in Florida?"

"Of course they do. And I've seen it on many menus. I just never asked what it was."

"It's squid."

"Squid!" she exclaimed, wrinkling her nose in distaste. "You mean like octopus?"

"N-not exactly," he returned, "but they're in the same family."

Samantha shivered. "I think I'll have clam sauce, if they have it."

"I'm sure they do."

In no time at all, Adam pushed open the door to what had to be the most beautiful restaurant she had ever been in. The foyer was a masterpiece in itself. Elegant love seats covered in exquisite tapestry and flanked by marble statues guarded the entrance to five spectacular dining rooms. Plush, rich carpeting, the color of wine and deep enough to sink into, made her feel like she was walking on a cloud.

Handmade Capodimonte chandeliers with crystal teardrops adorned the scenic-painted ceilings.

Very romantic, Samantha thought, taking it all in.

Very expensive, Adam groaned inwardly, taking a cursory look around him. It had been a while since he'd been here. They had obviously redecorated since that time. He fumbled through his pants pocket, hoping he had remembered to bring his American Express card. But the way his luck was running now, he was positive he *had* left home without it.

When the hostess approached them and asked if they had a reservation, Adam embarrassingly said no. But seeing that the luncheon crowd had already been seated, the hostess remarked that they were in luck and to follow her. As they weaved their way around the tables in one of the dining rooms, the hostess inquired if they'd like a table for two or an out-of-the-way romantic booth. Replying *booth* in unison, Samantha and Adam were soon seated in the far corner of the room.

Before she had a chance to remove her jacket, the maitre d' appeared. "Would you care for some wine?" he asked, placing the wine menu before them. Samantha looked at Adam shyly, "Mind if I have coffee instead? I didn't take the time to have breakfast, and all I'd need is a glass of wine and I'd be drunker than a skunk."

The maitre d' nodded. "Whatever the lady prefers. And you, sir?"

"Do it twice," Adam said, sighing. He really preferred the wine. Without looking up, he handed the menus back to the man.

When they were finally alone, Samantha leaned forward. "You didn't have to go along with my choice, you know. If you wanted wine you should have ordered it."

"That's okay," he said. "I didn't have breakfast either. We made the right choice."

While they were enjoying their coffee, Samantha raved at the beauty of the place. Each table was covered with a deep red linen cloth. Placed in the center was a Christmas floral arrangement with a lighted candle set in the middle. Matching the table cloth were red linen napkins rolled in wide, ornate silver holders. Giving Adam a sweet smile, Samantha picked up the menu in front of her. To her astonishment, she saw the entries were in Italian, and there were no prices listed.

Adam picked up on her reaction. "Don't worry," he grinned. "I can afford it. I'll simply hand over the deed to my house."

Usually that kind of statement would have made Samantha laugh, but at the moment, nothing amused her. In fact, what little appetite she had before had disappeared completely. She wished they had selected a restaurant far less elegant ... and less expensive. Closing the menu, she set it aside and remarked quietly, "Look, I'm really not very hungry. Could I possibly just have a sandwich?"

After going through all the trouble of trying to lift her spirits by bringing her here, Adam was livid, and he had a hard time keeping his anger under control. "If you had wanted a sandwich, why didn't you say so before we got here? I would have taken you to Wendy's."

He was right in being angry, and Samantha felt terrible. "I guess all that has happened has ruined my appetite. But you go ahead and order your spaghetti and squid. Only please don't get upset if I don't watch."

Adam slammed his menu down. When the waiter

appeared to take their orders, Samantha requested a chicken sandwich, plain, not toasted, with no lettuce and no fries on the side. She dared not look at Adam for fear that he might make a scene. Adam was seething, but he quietly ordered his spaghetti with extra calamari sauce to boot.

Halfway through the meal, Samantha announced she needed to visit the ladies' room. Adam wiped at his chin, and with his fork, pointed out that it was to the right, around the huge water fountain that graced the center of the room. Taking her purse in hand, she slid from the booth and had just circled the fountain when she froze in place, her unbelieving eyes taking in the burly figure of the man before her. There, staring her straight in the face, was Tony Garrett. Seated at a round table with five other men, Garrett stopped talking the moment they made eye contact. As a matter of fact, all conversation at the table came to an abrupt halt as the gentlemen first looked at Garrett, then at her. His face turned into a scowl, frightening Samantha so that she practically ran to escape him. She was afraid he'd embarrass her with his acid tongue in front of everyone in the crowded restaurant.

Once inside the ladies' room, she made a dash for the wall-length marble vanity. Every nerve in her body vibrated, while the blood in her veins rushed to her brain. She was certain her head was about to explode. Of all the restaurants in a city with millions of people, he had to have picked this one.

Turning on the cold water tap, Samantha picked up a neatly folded face cloth, dampened it, and blotted away the perspiration that ran down her face. Though it seemed to take forever, the color eventually returned to her cheeks. She didn't want to remain in there any longer, fearing Adam might think she'd become sick – which she almost had. Like it or not, it was time to leave her sanctuary before Adam sent the hostess in to check up on her.

That possibility alone was enough to make Samantha's knees stop knocking and her hands stop shaking. She reached into her purse for her lip gloss and touched it to her lips. Surprisingly, she began to feel confident and in control. And now, there was no doubt in her mind that she had the ability to pass right by Garrett as if he weren't there.

Dropping her lip gloss into her purse, she stepped to the door and pushed it open. Now she'd show him she couldn't be intimidated, she thought, walking with an easy stride that was more like a stroll.

With her head held high, she approached his table. Hooded blue eyes met tawny green, filling her with an invigorating feeling. Eat your heart out, big boy, she thought, moving to the right to pass him. Just as she did, she realized her purse was still open. Keeping her eyes straight ahead, she shut the clasp, oblivious to the fact that it had caught the edge of the tablecloth. Continuing on her way, she unknowingly dragged the tablecloth with her.

Piles of dishes, silverware, and glasses toppled over the men, covering them with wine and food. Still lost in her exhilaration, Samantha was unaware of the havoc taking place behind her. It was Garrett's roaring curse that brought her to a full stop seconds before the entire contents of the table came crashing to the floor.

Hearing the deafening sound, she spun around. Unbelieving eyes looked down at the tablecloth that was still wedged in her purse. She was so mortified, she was momentarily unable to move – to breathe. Somehow, her fingers managed to release the clasp and the tablecloth dropped to the floor.

Waiters, busboys, and patrons came running from everywhere to clean up the mess that could have only been made by Sam McCall.

She didn't return to Adam's table, but headed for the foyer, practically stumbling over her own feet in her haste to escape. Once there, Samantha's stomach did a somersault in her throat, and what little lunch she had eaten threatened to leave her right there. Dizziness came in rapid waves, causing the dimly-lit foyer to spin like a top, trapping her in its midst. Fortunately, there was a loveseat nearby. She dropped down upon it, bending her head low, disgrace and humiliation battling endlessly within her.

Adam entered the foyer. "You okay?" he asked, placing a comforting hand on her shoulder.

"Of course I'm not okay!" she snapped bitterly, pressing a tissue to her damp forehead. "I wish the floor would open up and swallow me. I'm as good as dead anyhow."

For the first time ever, Adam was at a loss for words, so he remained silent as he hovered over the distraught girl. Soon, he began to feel restless, so he moved away and began pacing before the entrance to the dining room. By now, he was at his wits end. He turned and said, "I'm going in there, locate the manager, and see what can be done about the damages. You wait here. I'll be right back with your jacket."

Samantha slowly raised her head. "Adam?" she called weakly, "Please tell Tony Garrett I'm sorry?"

"Sure," he muttered nervously as he straightened the knot in his tie. "That ought to make him feel much better."

When he left, she opened her purse and removed a

small tortoise-shelled mirror. Peering downheartedly at her pale reflection, she forced herself to regain her composure. "No sense in getting sick over this," she said out loud. "It was an accident. It could have happened to anyone. Surely when Adam extends my apologies, Tony Garrett will understand. He might even laugh at the incident and casually brush it off. Of course," she continued, feeling more secure now as she pinched her ashen cheeks and watched the color return, "that's exactly what he'll do. He'll regard the incident as humorous, and in his goodness, he'll let me live."

Concentrating on that uplifting thought, Samantha quickly pulled herself together. After returning the mirror to her purse, she rose to her feet. It was then that she heard footsteps approaching. Expecting it to be Adam, she adopted a confident smile and turned in the direction of the dining room. But when the tall, brawny figure marched into the foyer, the smile on Samantha's face froze, and once again the color drained from her cheeks. Feeling she might fall in a dead faint, she dropped back down onto the seat and watched, terrified, as Tony Garrett stepped toward her.

"Lucky me," he snarled, his voice low and insulting. "Killer McCall strikes again!" He stepped even closer, raking her with sardonic eyes. Samantha winced at his insolent gaze.

"I-I'm so very, very sorry," she apologized, staring at his once meticulous suit which now resembled an artist's palette. "It-it was an accident."

"Is *that* what it was?" Garrett spat vindictively. "I thought I'd been fingered by the mob!"

Samantha glowered back at him. "Listen here, Mr. Garrett, there's no need to be insulting! I said I was sorry.

Isn't that enough? Or perhaps you'd prefer I stamp it across my forehead in blood!"

"Now that's a satisfying suggestion," he sneered. Then inching even closer, he delivered the fatal blow. "You know, you remind me of Lizzie Borden – two dizzy dames with a single purpose – murder. Only Lizzie's weapon of choice was an ax. You still haven't decided–"

"I beg your pardon!" she snapped, interrupting him mid-sentence. She bolted to her feet.

"Oh, please," he mocked, "there's no need to beg. I consider myself lucky that I'm not leaving here on a stretcher."

"Ooooooh!" Samantha seethed as she watched him turn and leave the restaurant. She was still standing there when Adam returned. Her fists were clenched into balls of steel. Adam gave her a sidelong glance. "From the look on your face, I gather you two went another round." He helped her with her jacket, then slipped his hand beneath her elbow and led her towards the door.

Once outside, he sighed in relief. "That manager is one helluva guy. He wouldn't take a dime. Even Garrett refused my offer to have his suit cleaned. Personally, I think he should cut it up and use it to clean his car."

Still furious at Tony Garrett's merciless taunting, Samantha ignored Adam's chatter. "Of all the low-down, no-good, egotistical stuff shirts, that vicious clod beats them all!"

"Well, nobody's perfect," he said amusingly.

Samantha stopped dead in her tracks and shot an angry look his way. "You know, you're as much a buffoon as he is!"

"Hey, don't get touchy with me!" Adam declared

tightly, "right now I'm the only friend you've got!"

"Some friend you are," Samantha ridiculed, her voice rising with the resentment she now felt for him. "It's all your fault. If it hadn't been for you, I never would have met that creep!"

Adam became defensive. "First of all, that creep was pretty decent about the whole thing. And second, if it hadn't been for me, you'd still be an unknown writer hammering out your little thrillers, perhaps going nowhere. Now you're a principal character in a real life thriller, and you know what? You can't cut it!"

Samantha became incensed. "That's it! I'm going back to the hotel! I've had my quota of thrills and excitement for one day."

Adam retorted quickly, "Oh no you're not, young lady. You're going on to sign more books." He pulled her into the street and hailed an oncoming taxi. "You wanted fame? Well now you gotta work for it."

Twenty minutes later, Samantha found herself in Borders book store caught up in the same chaotic situation that had ensued at Barnes & Noble. Autograph hunters pounced upon her in throngs, each wanting the signature of the girl who had thrown Tony Garrett for a loop. Although grunting in silent fury, Samantha did what she had to do. She even went so far as to permit herself to be photographed with a glossy photo of Garrett held close to her smiling face. Hating every minute of it, Samantha inwardly vowed to be on the morning flight back to Tampa. She'd had enough of Adam Pearce, New York City, and especially Tony Garrett.

When the session was over, Samantha stood her ground and insisted on being taken back to the hotel. This time, Adam didn't protest. As the taxi drew to a stop, Adam

41

surprisingly invited her to dinner. The memory of their catastrophic lunch was still vivid in her mind, so she refused. "Thanks Adam, but no. I'm going to have a quiet supper in my room and work on my manuscript. I'm way behind as it is."

"Suit yourself," he said, "but don't forget, you're scheduled to appear on *Good Morning America* tomorrow morning at eight."

Samantha stiffened in her seat. "Get yourself another writer. I'm going home tomorrow."

The thread holding Adam's anger finally snapped. "You'll be at the television studio at seven-thirty sharp, if I have to deliver you there myself!"

Without saying another word, Samantha slammed the taxi door shut behind her and darted into the hotel. Later, after a light supper, she bathed lazily, turned on the television and scanned the stations. Nothing suited her, so she turned it off. She wasn't in the mood to write either, so she stretched out on her king size bed. After this gruesome day, it felt wonderful to relax.

No sooner had she snuggled into the depth of the soft pillow and closed her eyes, when her thoughts turned unconsciously to the restaurant and Tony Garrett. Strangely enough, she didn't try to banish his image from her mind, but rather took delight in remembering how his cool blue eyes had penetrated hers. Narrowed by his anger they had, nevertheless, sparkled with a brilliance that had rendered her helpless. His mouth was dangerously appealing as it mocked her relentlessly. He was everything the public claimed him to be, and in the restaurant that afternoon, his arrogant reputation had remained intact. Cool and aloof, he had looked upon her with baleful disgust, as if she were a serpent who deserved nothing more than to be crushed beneath his feet. Without warning, a teardrop began to roll down the side of her cheek in retrospect of what had to be the most humiliating moment of her life. It was then, as she lay coiled in a fetal position, that she pledged by all that was holy, to get even with that loathsome, despicable, yet irresistible man.

* * * * *

Samantha strolled into the studio at seven o'clock the following morning. Arriving thirty minutes early, her intent was to persuade Adam to arrange an appearance on the Tony Garrett Show. She knew Adam would be there long before air time, so she searched the various studios and was relieved to find him alone in the Green Room; a tiny den-like area set off from the main studio where the scheduled guests waited to be called on stage.

Poring over sheaves of paper, Adam didn't see her enter, so she softly cleared her throat to get his attention. Peering up at her from his spectacles, he broke out in a wide smile. "Cool."

"Do you really like the way I look, Adam?" she teased, twirling before him so that he was able to appreciate her loveliness from all angles. She had gotten up at 4:00 a.m. to prepare for this telecast. The appreciative look on Adam's face convinced her that her choice of a cream-colored suit and brown silk blouse draped in folds just above her breasts had been perfect. She had coiled her hair in a sophisticated twist that made her wide green eyes appear even larger, while a faint touch of blush on her cheekbones accentuated them to their fullest. Her small, full mouth was luscious with just a dab of gloss for appeal. With the exception of her wristwatch she wore no jewelry to detract from her chicness. She looked like a fashion model, poised, confident, and self-assured. More importantly, she felt as sure of herself as she looked.

Taking a seat beside him, she crossed her legs, and Adam's glasses nearly fogged as his gaze trailed upward beyond the hem of her skirt. "What are you trying to do?" he asked, staring at her legs, "raise the testosterone level of every guy in the building?"

"Could be," she taunted back, casting a narrow, sultry look his way.

Drawing his eyes back to his papers, he mumbled something inaudible to himself.

Samantha smiled cunningly at his uneasiness. "Actually, I dressed this way for my public. Now that I'm a *star*, I should look the part, don't you agree?"

Whatever was going on in that pretty little head of hers eluded Adam, but she had piqued his curiosity, and he couldn't wait to discover what she was up to. "Okay," he said with a sigh, dropping his papers onto an end table, "what's the reason for this sexy getup at seven in the morning?"

"I just told you," she teased. "Don't you believe me?"

"Sure I do," he said blandly. "I also believe in Santa Claus, the tooth fairy, and a little nymph named Tinkerbell." his eyes narrowed considerably. "I've got a sinking feeling you're out to nail Peter Pan."

"Bingo!" she exclaimed, a look of triumph in her sparkling green eyes. "And with a little help from you, Adam, Peter Pan will be feasting his baby blues on Sam McCall the class act, not Sam McCall the klutz."

44

"Ah," he said, finally grasping her message. "So Tony Garrett's your little guy in the green suit. I shoulda guessed. I know this is a crazy question, and I'm gonna regret asking it, but how am I supposed to help?"

Her voice was sweet and charming. "I want you to call him and persuade him to watch the show."

"Why?" he asked tensely.

"Because I want to be invited back on *his* show."

"Why?" he repeated. "Haven't you had enough?"

"Oh yes, my friend," she hissed, remembering the way he had degraded her in the restaurant. "I've had more than enough. But that man hasn't seen the last of me. He's got to pay for the way he insulted me yesterday and the night before. But first, I wanted to set the bait. If he's normal, he'll bite. Then once I get there, I'll let him have it with both barrels. He'll never know what hit him."

"Personally, I still don't think he knows what hit him. Nevertheless, do you really believe you can pull this little caper off by showing him some cleavage and shapely gams?" He laughed heartily. "It won't work, Killer. Better than you have tried and failed. I know. I've seen some pros in action. You're forgetting he's surrounded by beauties all the time. Here in the Big Apple, they're a dime a dozen. Besides, you two have locked horns twice already. I don't care if you walk out on stage in your birthday suit. He's not gonna take the bite."

"He will if you convince him that our combativeness is what those bloodthirsty viewers want to see. Plus, think of the ratings. Isn't that what his show is all about?"

Adam considered it for a moment, then asked, "Have you forgotten your statement about making a return appearance *only* if he makes a public apology?" She answered without hesitating. "Of course I haven't forgotten. I've simply changed my mind. Woman's prerogative, you know. I'm willing to appear without it." Suddenly her eyes flashed with fire, and her lips curled in annoyance. "I don't care how you do it Adam, just *do* it! I've got to get back on that show!"

Adam gathered his papers, rose from his seat, and sighed. "Okay, okay. I'll see what I can do. Just don't make matters worse by slinging mud at him on this program." Then, sputtering something about a death wish, he left the room, leaving the door ajar. While he was gone, one of the show's co-hosts appeared and handed Samantha a copy of her book. Ten minutes later she took her seat on stage.

When the show was over, Samantha shook hands with the crew and returned to the Green Room. Adam Pearce was waiting for her. Sitting with one leg dangled over the arm of his chair, he watched her approach him. His face was expressionless, yet it spoke volumes. "No dice, huh?" she asked, disappointment evident in her voice.

"Sorry, Red," he mumbled, raking his slim fingers through his salt and pepper-colored hair. "I called his producer, but his show is going into reruns for the next couple of weeks because of the holidays. However, the guy said he'd try to hunt Garrett down and suggest he watch the show, but he couldn't give me any guarantees. I watched it here on the monitor. You looked great." He gave her a sly little wink. "Your legs looked great, too. Now let's get out of here. I could use some breakfast."

Soon after, they were settling into their seats in a small café in Rockefeller Center. Adam had claimed it was one of his favorite spots. It wasn't difficult for Samantha to understand why. The café overlooked an enormous skating rink where brightly clad skaters whirled and twirled before the admiring glances of the diners. Ordinarily, Samantha's eyes would have been glued to the skaters, for she had always envied anyone who could remain upright on those slim silver blades for more than five minutes without landing awkwardly on their bottoms. But the artistry displayed before her was lost in the disappointment she still felt at not having the chance to reappear on Garrett's show.

Adam's keen senses were attuned to her disappointment. As soon as the waiter set their coffee cups before them, he remarked compassionately, "You can't win 'em all, girl. You gave it your best shot. It just isn't in the cards."

Samantha stirred her coffee vigorously. "I can't go home without settling the score, Adam. I just can't."

His mouth stretched into a grim line. "It seems to me you're ahead in this game. You whacked him on stage, you've defended that action on the news, and you decorated him with enough food to feed the troops in Iraq. It's a wonder he hasn't put out a contract on your pretty little head." His eyes lowered in skepticism. "Could it be that you want to get on his show for *another* reason?"

"What's that supposed to mean?" she shot back.

"I think you've fallen for him. You wouldn't be the first. He's got female hearts palpitating all over the country. Women love him. He's charged with animal magnetism, just like me." He threw his head back and laughed heartily, but instead of joining him in his bit of fun, Samantha suddenly became oddly curious about the clown-like man who sat opposite her.

Unlike Tony Garrett, Adam Pearce did not exude animal magnetism. At best, he stood five feet five inches tall and weighed no more than one hundred forty pounds. His fine salt and pepper-colored hair fell listlessly over a deeply creviced brow. Above his thin-lipped mouth was a short, straight mustache, and behind round silver-framed glasses were deeply set, twinkling brown eyes. Samantha guessed his age to be about forty-five. But then glancing at his well-kept, slightly-built frame, she admitted he could have been younger.

Sipping his coffee, he looked at her square in the eyes. Somehow he knew she was assessing him. He cleared his throat and smoothed the hair at his temples. Then, with a broad smile he queried, "You see it, too, don't you?"

"See what?" she returned.

"My animal magnetism, what else?"

Samantha couldn't help but laugh. Whatever Adam lacked physically, he made up for with his quick wit. And now, gazing back at him, she wondered if that keen sense of humor was a mask of defense, a false face he put on before her and the world. It prompted her to ask him point blank, "Adam, are you married?"

He raised and fluttered his thin eyebrows in a bad imitation of Groucho Marx. "Why? What did you have in mind?"

"Be serious, Adam. I really want to know."

Ever so slowly, the smile faded from his lips. He lowered his eyes to his cup. "I *was* married," he said. "And I had a son. But I lost them both about ten years ago."

Samantha instantly regretted having asked the question. "I'm sorry, Adam. I had no idea. Yet, I can certainly relate to your loss."

Adam gave her a strange look. "Why do you say that?"

"Because I lost my husband, too. Only we never had children." Her eyes filled, and she looked away from him. She didn't particularly want to talk about Jack and the way he died, but she could sense, by Adam's intense stare, that he wanted to know the details of her past that now seemed to bond them together in a nonprofessional way.

He tried to lighten the heaviness of the conversation by resorting to one of his usual comedic quips. "I'll tell you my tale of woe, if you'll tell me yours. Of course, you really don't have to. I'll understand."

"No, no," she answered, gathering her composure by taking in a heavy breath. "I married Jack a little over five years ago when I was twenty-five. We lived near my folks in Buffalo, New York. Jack was a state trooper. We were married only four months when he was involved in an accident on the Thruway. A drunk driver hit his patrol car, and he was killed instantly. Because we were married for such a short time and had no kids, I resumed my maiden name, McCall, and moved back home. Jack had a substantial life insurance policy that allowed me to quit my job as a court stenographer and devote all my time to writing. My dad is a retired police captain. His arthritis nearly cripples him in the winter, so we spend them in Tampa. Then we go back to Buffalo in the spring. End of story. Now, how about you?"

Listening to her, Adam marveled at her control and acceptance of her fate. Five years ago, he was still a basket case. He took a gulp of coffee. "I was fixing up our cabin on Hunter Mountain, up in the Catskills. My wife and son were at home on Long Island. They were supposed to join me, but there was an accident at the house. A fire..." His voice trembled off, belying his calm demeanor. When he lifted his gaze to Samantha's somber face, he said, "You remind me so much of her. She was tiny, had red hair, was a spit-fire like you, and ironically enough, she dabbled in mystery writing. She never intended to publish anything, even though I thought her work was commendable.

"At that time, I was an editor for another publishing house, but after they died, I decided to make a complete change in my life, so I ventured out on my own as an agent. When you wrote to me and asked me to represent you, I got this incredible urge to do for you what I couldn't do for her. I want you to be a success, perhaps more than you do. It's become a personal obsession with me, just as Garrett has become a personal obsession with you."

Samantha felt the color rise in her cheeks. Was that what Garrett had become to her? An obsession? True, she had gone to great lengths to make herself especially attractive for this morning's show. Bait, she had called it. Bait meant to charm the most uncharming man she had ever met. But did she really believe her shapely legs and sophisticated attire would turn his head? A man who was used to having women bare all before him? And for what? To get back at him for treating her so horribly? Or was Adam right when he said she had fallen in love with him? And if so, what chance did she stand against the beauties that constantly threw themselves at his feet? He was a man who could pick and choose his women at will.

Taking all that into consideration, Samantha knew he would *never* fall for a clumsy little mystery writer who had committed the unpardonable sin of making a fool of him on national television.

Lost in deep thought, Samantha was unaware that Adam was speaking to her.

"I'm sorry, Adam. What did you say?"

"I said, I have to go. I have a meeting in half an hour."

"Good." She dabbed at the corners of her mouth with her napkin. "I'm heading over to Fifth Avenue to do some Christmas shopping. Then I'm going back to the hotel and pack. My flight to Tampa leaves at seven-thirty tomorrow morning."

CHAPTER FOUR

The desk clerk spotted Samantha awkwardly maneuvering her way through the hotel doors. Arms filled with shopping bags and packages, she stopped when he called out that she had an urgent message. Groaning inwardly, Samantha headed for the desk, thinking everything about her life these days was urgent. "Is it from a man named Adam Pearce?" she asked, peering over her packages.

"I believe that's the gentleman's name," he replied, holding the message in his scrawny little hand.

With her nose, she pointed to the bag at the top of the heap and said, "Drop it in here, please, I'm a bit bogged down, as you can see."

"Certainly," he replied, displaying the same dumb grin he had the night she'd returned from the studio. She was tempted to ask if he was working a triple shift or owned the place, seeing he was always at the desk no matter what time of day it was. But she held her tongue and smiled as he tucked the slip of paper into the bag marked Lord & Taylor.

Thankfully, the doors to the elevator parted just as she approached it. Once inside, she took the tip of her key and pressed the button to the tenth floor. Out of curiosity, she glanced toward the man before the doors closed. Just as she had expected, the desk clerk was watching her, his silly grin still fixed on his face. She lowered the packages just enough to give him a coy little wink. "That should give him a rise," she muttered out loud, right before the doors closed.

"Not as much as these did," came a sultry female

voice behind her.

Samantha blushed. She hadn't realized she wasn't alone. Turning slightly, she half-gasped at the Amazon-like creature in the corner. "See what I mean?" said the woman who was at least six feet tall and had yellow bleached blonde, over-teased hair. Samantha stared in awe when the blonde unbuttoned her red blazer and revealed a see-through white shell top that was a good two sizes too small. The woman's breasts were the size of cantaloupes, and she flashed them into Samantha's face with pride.

"Guess we both made his day," she said as the elevator stopped at the tenth floor. When the doors finally parted, the two attempted to step into the hall at the same time. But Samantha's packages and the woman's voluptuous chest wedged them together so that neither of them could move. By now, the two were in hysterics. Giving a nod, the blonde stepped back to let Samantha pass.

Her laughter still permeated through the hall as she unlocked the door and entered her room. Dying to be rid of her shoes, Samantha kicked them off. Her arms were aching from the weight of her gifts, so she gently placed them on the bed. When she did, the note from Adam slid out of the bag and sailed to the floor. Samantha saw it but ignored it. Whatever it was could wait. Right now she was starving. It didn't take her long to undress, climb into her warm robe and slippers, then dial room service for a sandwich and a large pot of coffee.

As soon as she finished her lunch, she began to open the presents, giggling excitedly as she examined each one. At Tiffany's, she had selected gold hooped earrings for her mother, and a solid gold lighter for her father's pipe. At Saks Fifth Avenue, she had chosen shoulder-strap Gucci bags for her two sisters, and an extra piece of luggage to carry them home in. But the piece de resistance was a pink peignoir she had purchased for herself. She had fallen in love with the soft, flowing, see-through gown the moment she laid eyes on it. It had cost a king's ransom, but Samantha didn't care. It had been a long time since she'd bought anything so extravagant for herself, and she was going to see to it that she and her family had the best Christmas ever. She was finally going home, leaving behind New York City, Adam, and of course ... Tony Garrett.

Strange, but part of her felt sad at that thought. She had tried her best to finagle a return appearance on his show, to get back at him. That's what she told herself and Adam. But Adam didn't buy the excuse. And now, suddenly, neither did she. Life sure has its twists and turns, she thought, placing the peignoir back into its box. It also had its reasons. So what was the purpose fate had in mind when it brought the two of them together? Surely it had not intended...

A loud rapping at the door brought Samantha back to reality.

"Don't you know what *urgent* means?" Adam snapped the instant Samantha opened the door. He rushed passed her, eyed the gifts on the bed, then turned abruptly to face her. "How long have you been back?"

Samantha pulled a face. "What difference does it make? I've finished my business here in New York, so what could possibly be so urgent?"

Adam knew there was no way to soften the blow, so he quickly blurted out, "You're not going back to Florida tomorrow."

"Excuse me?" She was sure she had heard him

correctly, but in case she hadn't, she needed support under her. She dropped down onto the bed. He came and sat beside her. "I'm sorry, Red, but you're not going home."

"Says who?"

"Bob Fields, that's who. He wants your manuscript by Christmas."

Samantha became incensed. "My deadline is January second. I promised him he'd have it then, and he will!"

"Not by the looks of those presents," Adam retorted. If you go home tomorrow, you'll get caught up in the holiday festivities. He knows it and so do I. It's only natural. So, I've come up with a plan where you can write undisturbed for the next twelve days. The following morning will be Christmas Eve. I'll come and get you with plane tickets in my pocket. You'll be home for Christmas without having to worry about the manuscript, and everybody will be happy."

Samantha got to her feet and stared down at him. "You've got it all figured out, haven't you? Nice of you to consult me. And where am I supposed to work? Locked up here in this hotel room?"

"No, my dear. I'm going to take you up to my cabin on Hunter Mountain in the Catskills. You'll have everything you need, and you won't be isolated. There are cabins all around the place. My car is downstairs, loaded with food. We'll pick up some perishables on the way. But we have to leave now because it's a four hour drive, and I want it to still be light when we get there. Now, hurry and get packed." From the tone of his voice, Samantha knew it would be futile to argue with him. She was ready in twenty minutes.

* * * * *

By the time Adam's car drew to a halt before the tiny rustic cabin, Samantha was ready to scream. The heater in his vintage red Volkswagen had conked out on the outskirts of the city, and now, some four hours later, Samantha's fingers and toes were tingling with numbness. Her gaze swept down to her open-toed, high-heel shoes, then out the side window and beyond the snow-covered terrain.

"I hope you're prepared to carry me into the cabin," she declared hotly, fixing her stormy green eyes on him. Adam swung open the car door and said in jest, "If I did that, we'd have to call the paramedics."

"Cute," she snapped through clenched teeth as she watched Adam walk around to her side. He opened the door and poked his head inside. "I've got an old pair of boots somewhere in the cabin. I suppose you're gonna sit here like Cinderella until I bring them out and slip them on your dainty little feet like Prince Charming."

"Never mind!" she flared, shoving him back. Then she swung her feet past him and planked them into the frigid white mounds. "Oh, God!" she exclaimed loudly as her feet disappeared into the snow. "It's freezing! *I'm* freezing! Take me back to the city. I'll work in the hotel room!"

"Too late now, twinkle toes," Adam called with a laugh, plodding his way towards the door.

Fuming out loud, yet following closely behind, Samantha slipped and slid, nearly falling twice before stepping into the cold, dark, dust-filled cabin. When Adam stopped before a plaid high-back sofa, he glanced around the room, opened his arms wide and said lightheartedly, "Be it ever so humble–"

"...there's no place like Florida," she finished, casting

56

a downhearted look at her surroundings. "No wonder my family waves sayonara to Buffalo every winter. Who needs this? I must have been crazy to give in to your little scheme. Although the truth is, I really didn't give in. I was kidnapped!"

Adam turned on his heels to face her. "Where's your sense of adventure, girl?" he asked, dusting off the snow from his trousers. "You're in the heart of the great outdoors. You got your snow and your mountains and your clean fresh air. Once you get used to romping in the snow, you'll trade in your golf clubs and mint juleps for skis and a hot toddy."

"Never!" she growled, stomping her feet angrily on a small braided rug to shake the snow from her slacks and shoes. Samantha's companion ignored her grunting as he moved around the room, pushing the short damask curtains away from the windows. Immediately, the room became bathed in sunlight. Whistling a happy tune, he began to load the red brick fireplace with logs that were stacked beside it in a wide iron basket. As soon as he set a match to them, an inviting warmth lured Samantha from her place on the rug.

"That's more like it," she said, twisting her hands together in front of the roaring fire. It didn't take long before the heat penetrated through her chilled bones, so she removed her jacket and tossed it over the arm of the brightly plaid sofa, thinking this arrangement might not be so bad after all. In fact, she was feeling quite adventurous, so she began to explore what was now her new home for the next twelve days.

The room with the hearth served as both kitchen and living room. Divided by a knotty pine counter with three ladder back chairs, the kitchen area boasted a small refrigerator, an electric stove, and a round maple table with four matching captain's chairs. Knotty pine cabinets lined the walls above and below the stainless steel sink, and a large wool braided rug covered the hardwood floor beneath.

Returning to the living room area, she noticed a barn wood china cabinet to the left of the hearth, and a matching roll-top desk to the right. An ottoman covered in the same plaid material as the couch was positioned beside it. At the opposite end stood a square end table with a brown ginger jar lamp. Above all this country charm was a white ceiling with thick wooden beams.

"Like it?" Adam queried, moving past her to the kitchen where he filled a kettle with water and set it on the stove. For all her misgivings, Samantha had to admit the cabin was cozy and quite alluring. She had never been to a mountain retreat before, having only seen photographs of them in magazines. Now she would be temporarily living in one, and to be honest, she was beginning to look forward to it. The only drawback was the fact that she would be occupying this intimate little hideaway alone. Too bad, she thought, as she gazed at the fire feeling disappointed. But she had come here to work, not to fantasize about herself being snowbound with the man who got away...

"Earth to McCall," Adam beckoned, waving his hand in front of her dazed eyes. Samantha laughed. "I'm mesmerized by that fire. It's fabulous." Then she looked towards the stove. "What's the water for?"

"I thought we'd share a quick cup of instant coffee before I left," he said as he buttoned his coat and turned towards the door. "While it's heating, I'll go and get your luggage and groceries from the car. Make yourself comfortable."

When Adam returned, he set the supplies in the

cabinets and refrigerator, showed Samantha where everything was, then led her into the bedroom which was off to the side of the kitchen. The room was exceptionally small, its contents consisting of a twin bed, a small maple bureau with a frameless mirror above, and a tiny closet where the blankets and linens were kept. Then urging her to look out the room's only window, he pointed to a shed which was attached to the cabin.

"In there is a pile of wood that should last you until I get back," he said with confidence. "I suggest at the start of the day you bring several logs inside and set them in the basket. The shed gets damp from the snow. That way the wood will be dry enough to burn. Got it?"

"Yes, I think so," she answered with less confidence than Adam.

Positioned just off to the left of the bed was a wood burning stove. Samantha voiced her ignorance in using one. She had never lit a fireplace as well, but she refused to admit her inability to care for both sources of heat.

Adam steered clear of the stove. "Don't concern yourself with that," he said offhandedly. "It would be best if you didn't use this room at all. The sofa opens out into a bed, so you can sleep in the living room. That way you'll only have to bother with the hearth." After that, he stepped around her and opened a door beside the maple bureau. "This is the bath. It has baseboard heat to keep you and the pipes from freezing."

Placing his hand under her elbow, he led her from the room and closed the door behind them. After he had fixed the coffee and poured it into tall mugs, he sat down on the sofa. Samantha chose to drink hers standing before the fire. "When I looked out the bedroom window, I noticed another cabin about a hundred yards away," she said, pursing her lips. "There's smoke coming from the chimney, so it's occupied. Do you know who's staying there?"

"I'm glad you mentioned that," he said, gulping the last of his drink. "It belongs to a guy named Jack Whitman. He's the executive vice-president of Station WINZ. He vacations here with his family every winter. Seems to me I already told you there were cabins nearby, so you'll have someone to turn to should a problem arise. But I don't anticipate any." He set his mug on the end table and rose to his feet. "I'd better be heading back. But before I go, I have an apology to make. I forgot to bring along my cell phone. You don't happen to have one with you, do you?"

"No." Samantha sighed. "I packed so fast, I left it back home. So how am I supposed to tell my family where I am or get in touch with you if I need to?"

Adam answered smoothly, "I'll call your folks for you as soon as I get back to the city. And, if you need me, just take your little body up to Jack's place. I'm sure he has a phone. Now, I'd better get going."

Samantha walked him to the door. Just before he opened it, Adam turned to her and placed both hands on her shoulders. "Do you have enough battery packs for your laptop, just in case?" he asked, his eyes purposely avoiding hers. She sensed he was keeping something from her, something he didn't want her to know.

"Look at me, Adam," she said nervously. "What do you mean, just in case?"

Adam gave a forced chuckle. "I didn't mean to alarm you. It's just that you're in the mountains now, and it snows occasionally. Oftentimes when it does, the power goes out, so you may have to rely on your battery packs. Also, I'm sure you've noticed there's no TV. We ... ah ... that is, my family never wanted one here. But there's a radio with a cassette player and an ample supply of batteries in the bottom of the china cabinet, so you can listen to the news and some music." He gave her a peck on the cheek before he turned to open the door. "Remember that you're here to work. Bob Fields wants that manuscript, and I went out on a limb to try and accommodate everyone concerned. The fewer distractions you have, the better. Take care and keep your little nose to the grindstone. The next time you see me you'll be Florida-bound, and I'll have your completed manuscript." He heaved a sigh. "Then we'll *all* have a Merry Christmas."

When he left, Samantha stepped over to the window and forced herself to give him a smile and a hearty wave goodbye. She was glad he wasn't near enough to see the smile was not genuine. How could it be? She wasn't happy to see him go, because for some inexplicable reason, all her instincts told her that he would *not* be back on Christmas Eve.

Her heartbeat picked up speed as she watched him drive away. Sure he would, she said inwardly, trying to convince herself that she was wrong. Adam would never let her down.

No sooner did that disturbing thought pop into her mind, when a myriad of unanswerable questions began replacing it. Had she done the right thing by giving in and coming here? Was she really safe? Could one of the cabins nestled in the clump of trees in the distance be harboring a fugitive from justice? Or worse yet, a homicidal maniac who lured his victims to his bungalow, massacred them, then buried them in the snow? A seedy looking villain in one of her short stories had done it. So what made her think fate didn't have her same demise in mind for her?

"Really, girl," she said aloud as she drew the curtains closed against the setting sun. "Keep thinking thoughts like that, and you'd better switch to writing cookbooks instead of thrillers. You're scaring yourself to death." What she needed to do to calm herself was to get busy. In less than a heartbeat, she turned on all the lights, then searched the bottom of the china closet, looking for the radio. When she found it, she scanned the stations until she found one that played soft, soothing music. The combination of the roaring fire and the melodious tunes did the trick.

She took her luggage and gifts into the bedroom, unpacked her things, and hung her clothes in the closet. She was so busy keeping busy that she had forgotten the time. Her stomach growled. She checked the watch on her wrist and saw it was almost six o'clock. She still had plenty of time to eat, then tackle the last chapter she was working on. With four more to go, she knew she had her work cut out for her.

The travel alarm on the end table read 11:45. Time to call it a night. Snuggled warmly in the sofa bed, she gave an exhausted sigh. With the chapter finished, the fire burning brightly, and five remaining logs in the basket, the last thought she had before drifting off was ... what a waste of a beautiful night.

* * * * *

For the next twelve days she kept to the routine she had mapped out for herself. First thing in the morning before breakfast, she'd pull on Adam's old black rubber boots, trudge out to the shed, fill her arms with logs, then carry the wood back to the cabin. On this particular day, before she closed the door to the shed, she counted the logs. There were twenty. *That should hold me until Adam comes,* she thought happily. What made her even happier was the fact that it hadn't snowed in the time she was there. Each day, sunlight filled the room, and not a soul had passed by the windows to break her concentration. By four o'clock in the afternoon, she finished her manuscript. Adam was right, as usual. This would be a merry Christmas for everyone after all.

She fixed herself a light supper, then decided not to wait until morning to gather the remaining logs. She'd bring them in tonight, allowing the extra time to repack her clothes and gifts. She was so thrilled at the thought of going home that she didn't mind putting on the ugly black boots. By this time tomorrow she'd be wearing sandals and giggling along with her family as they opened their presents. Her gaiety was short-lived.

The moment she opened the shed door, she gave a strangled cry. Someone had stolen the logs! What was she going to do now? She had put three on the fire as soon as she got up. There were only six left. That would never get her through the day and night.

Even though the air was freezing, Samantha could feel beads of sweat trickle down the back of her neck, and her heart pounded furiously in her chest. This was not the time to panic, she told herself. If she did run out of logs, she would simply turn up the thermostat. There was still plenty of coffee. She would survive. Still, she couldn't imagine who would do such a thing. If someone in one of the cabins nearby needed wood, he could have at least had the courtesy to ask to borrow some.

Furious, she slammed the shed door shut behind her and looked around. Not surprised, she saw tracks in the snow. Tracks made by a sled. She wrapped her jacket tightly around herself and followed the trail across the terrain down a small hill to a clump of trees. At this point she was forced to stop. Whoever took the wood had done an expert job of wiping away the tracks, along with their footprints. There was no way of judging which way she should go.

"Wait until I tell Adam what great neighbors he has," she said out loud as she stomped back to the cabin. Still fuming, she threw off her jacket and stepped before the fire, angrily rubbing her hands together to warm them. The flames were beginning to turn to ashes, and it was only five-thirty. Even if Adam left New York at dawn as planned, he wouldn't arrive until around nine ... maybe. "Damn," she cursed. Why had she forgotten to bring her cell phone!

Totally at a loss as to what to do, she considered trudging to one of the cabins nearby, then quickly changed her mind. If she'd only calm down and think things through, she'd find a way to keep the flames going.

Paper and boxes. That's what she needed. Anything to keep from using the wood. Like a whirlwind, she raced through the entire cabin, gathering up her gift boxes along with a bunch of Adam's outdated *Time* magazines she'd found in a carton on the bottom of the bedroom closet. "Sorry, pal," she said, dragging them to the front of the hearth. "In case you haven't read them, I'll give you the scoop on everything, including Liz Taylor's newest husband and diet. Sad to say, neither of them worked."

Trying her best to relax, she began casting one magazine after another onto the dying flames. When she was through, she went into the bedroom, packed everything into the suitcase, then returned to the living room where she began to tear at the gift boxes and cast them into the fire. The flames blazed. She didn't know how long it would last, so she thought it best if she stayed dressed and went to bed. Anything to keep warm.

She didn't expect sleep to come, and it didn't. She was far too nervous to sleep. Not only that, she was beginning to feel chilly despite the roaring fire, so she decided to turn up the thermostat even higher. She hopped out of bed and began searching for it. It was just above the counter that separated the two rooms. When she went to turn the dial to its highest setting, she found it was already there, and yet the temperature in the room was a mere fifty-two degrees.

"That can't be right," she said out loud, dashing into the bathroom. When she touched the heater, it was barely warm against her fingers. More than likely, the temperature outside must have dropped to below zero and the drafty cabin couldn't handle it. So much for high hopes.

Realizing she had no other alternative but to put the remaining logs into the fire or freeze to death, she gently placed them in the hearth. In minutes, the room was once again toasty warm. Exhausted to the quick, she climbed into bed and fell asleep as her head hit the pillow.

* * * * *

Was she dreaming or did she hear something go *pop*? Her eyes flew open and darted around the darkened room. It didn't take a rocket scientist to figure out that danger had now made its way inside the cabin. Deep in the pit of her stomach she felt it, and it terrified her. The fire in the hearth had gone out without leaving so much as a burning ember. Instinctively, she knew the problem facing her now was much more perilous than anything she had anticipated.

She slid to the edge of the sofa and switched on the lamp. Nothing happened. Shaking all over, she sent up a silent prayer that the problem was nothing more than a burned-out light bulb. She knew there were some in the kitchen cabinet, so she swung her legs off the sofa only to plank them into ankle-deep water. She let out a spine-chilling shriek as terror shook her. She was afraid to move, but she had no choice. Obviously, the cabin had lost its electricity and the pipes had burst.

Drawing her stocking feet back onto the sofa, she quickly put on her jacket. Next to come were the boots. Reaching down to get them, she discovered they were soaked to the brim. Drying them off on the blankets, she slid into them and fastened the metal clips with trembling fingers. Groaning audibly, she sloshed her way into the bedroom and grabbed her suitcase. She would take her belongings and tread over to Jack Whitman's cabin to call Adam, feeling even worse at having to trouble the Whitman family at two o'clock in the morning.

With only a jacket and boots to ward off the cold, she waded quickly to the door. As soon as she unfastened the latch, a blustering gust of wind and ice pellets threw open the door, stinging her eyes and obscuring her vision. Clad in her skimpy attire, she was painfully aware of the possibility she'd freeze to death before making it to the cabin. She was too tiny, too fragile to do battle with a blizzard of this intensity, yet she had to get there. With each step she took, it became harder to breathe. The wind and snow thrashed her around like a rag doll. She could feel her ears and hands becoming frostbitten. She was too terrorized to cry, to think, even to pray. The Whitman cabin may have been only yards away, but to Samantha it seemed like a million miles.

"Please...please..." she whispered as she finally reached her destination. Giving the door a weak rap with her numbed fist, she collapsed into the arms of the man who opened the door.

CHAPTER FIVE

Something made her nose itch. Something irritating, like a loose piece of thread. Her arms felt like leaden weights requiring all the strength she could muster just to move her hand to her nose. When it finally got there, Samantha found the culprit to be the ruffled edge of a quilt. She gently pushed it away and slowly opened her eyes. Still unable to focus properly, she closed her eyes again.

"I apologize for interrupting your sleep, Mr. Whitman," she slurred. "I hope I haven't inconvenienced your family, but..."

"Shhh," he whispered gently. "Don't try to talk. You need your rest. You've been through quite an ordeal."

The sound of his voice made Samantha shake her head in a valiant fight to push through the fog in her brain. Was she imagining it, or did his voice sound distinctly familiar? Eyes still closed, she asked timidly, "Maybe I'm hallucinating, but I know your voice. Have we ever met?"

"Yes, we have," he answered. "Twice, to be exact."

Twice, he had said. *Twice*, she repeated to herself. Suddenly it registered. Once in a television studio and again in a restaurant. Dear God, she prayed, please let me be dreaming. This couldn't possibly be... This time her eyes flew open. Tony Garrett!

As if a bomb had been set off behind her, Samantha jutted forward, forgetting about the quilt. It dropped to her lap, exposing her naked breasts to his view. Thoroughly flustered, not to mention embarrassed, she snatched the covering and raised it high beneath her chin.

"What are *you* doing here?" she gasped. "This place is supposed to belong to a man named Jack Whitman! Don't tell me I got lost!"

Tony Garrett smiled and sat down beside her on the sofa bed. Samantha watched him drink her in with his cool blue eyes, making her feel dizzy. The last time his eyes met hers, they were shooting fireworks. She'd felt dizzy that time as well.

"No, you're not lost, Samantha," he said, keeping his eyes locked with hers. You're exactly where you're supposed to be."

His comment threw her into a state of total confusion. "Did I miss something?"

Now that she was here, Garrett knew it was time she was told the truth ... which wasn't going to be easy. Having already witnessed her unbridled temper, he knew she'd be furious. Hopefully, when he finished, she'd forgive him and understand. If she didn't, he'd make her understand. He knew by the way she was looking at him that she had feelings for him. The question was, did they go as deep as his feelings for her?

With his warm body so close, Samantha's already foggy mind got foggier. His clean masculine scent filled her senses, making her heart do somersaults in her chest. Without a doubt, he was the handsomest, sexiest man she'd ever seen. For a brief moment she recalled how she'd prodded Adam to bring them together, using a return appearance on his show as an excuse to see him again. In her wildest dreams she never imagined that one day she would end up lying naked in his bed. Nevertheless, she wanted an answer to her question, and she wanted it now. Propping herself up on her elbow, she looked directly into

69

his eyes. "If I'm exactly where I'm supposed to be, then you've got some explaining to do. So get to it."

Garrett's lips moved in a half grin as he brazenly stretched out beside her and leaned his head on the back of the sofa. "For starters, I wish you'd drop the formalities and call me Tony. After all, I've seen you naked, and lady, I like what I saw."

Samantha turned crimson. "Never mind that!" she quipped, trying to ignore the fact that his admission made her nipples go hard. She was thankful he couldn't see them through the thickness of the quilt.

For a minute or two he couldn't see anything. He was too preoccupied with the fire that was burning in his groin. He had all he could do to keep from throwing off the quilt and taking her right there.

"I'm waiting."

Garrett held himself in check by focusing on her liquid green eyes. "The day you appeared on *Good Morning America*, Adam Pearce phoned me and suggested I give you a return shot on my show. I told him I wanted more time with you than that. He said he had a cabin on Hunter Mountain, and that our mutual friend, Jack Whitman, had one near it. Pearce also knew that Whitman would be taking his family to the Bahamas for the holidays, instead of coming here this year, so Pearce called him, got the okay for me to use his place, then promised he'd get you up here."

"How clever of him," she retorted. "Did he also arrange to have someone steal my firewood, then top it off with a blizzard?"

"N-not exactly."

"Then what exactly?"

"It was my idea to take the wood, along with the ax, I

might add. Knowing you, you'd have probably chopped down a couple of trees. You've got a mighty powerful arm there for someone so tiny."

His confession was becoming more interesting by the minute. "So you took my wood. So what? The cabin has electric heat, and Adam is expected to arrive in the morning."

"Apparently you don't have a radio."

"Samantha straightened her spine. "Yes I do."

Garrett threw back his head and laughed heartily. "Then I guess you don't listen to the local weather, because if you had, you would have known that a blizzard was due to hit the mountains tonight. Looks like the weatherman was right on the money. He also saved me a second trip to your place."

"How do you figure that?"

"Simple," he answered. "When a blizzard hits, the area always loses its electricity. I knew you had no wood, and Pearce admitted he had no backup generator. Eventually you'd lose your power, so that by morning you'd be half-frozen to death .Fortunately for me, Whitman had a back-up generator. So about an hour ago I was about to head over to your place to rescue you, when suddenly there was a rap on my door, and there you were, suitcase and all. I caught you just as you passed out. I removed your clothes, which were stuck to you, and quickly got you under the quilt. I even got you to sip some brandy. You don't remember that, do you?"

Samantha was silent for a moment. She couldn't understand why he had wanted more time with her after what she had put him through. Perhaps his initial intentions were to do her harm by torturing her mentally and physically, bit by bit, like first taking her wood. Then, with no electricity to keep her warm, he wouldn't have had to do anything else. Knowing the blizzard was coming, all he had to do was wait for her to die from hypothermia, and she would have been finally out of his life. So why the rescue act?

When she didn't answer him, he repeated the question. "No," she whispered. "I don't remember a thing. Guess I should thank you for saving my life."

He threw her a loop by saying, "Believe me, it was my pleasure." And it certainly was. He had given thanks that she couldn't see him lusting over her slender body with her breasts small but full, her tiny waist, flat belly, and legs he had ached from day one to feel wrapped around him. Just thinking about it was causing him to get hard again, so he got up from the sofa and placed several logs on the fire. He waited for his manhood to relax before stripping off his clothes, leaving them in a heap on the rug. Standing stark naked before her horrified eyes, he watched her gawk as he pulled back the quilt and said, "I'm beat. I'm going to sleep."

"Not in this bed!" she flared indignantly, clutching the quilt so tightly, her knuckles turned white.

Garrett ignored her protest and smiled as he slid his magnificent body beneath the quilt. After resting his dark head on the back of his forearm, he turned slightly towards her and muttered wickedly, "What's the matter, little lady? Afraid you won't be able to keep your hands off me?"

That was exactly what she was afraid of, but she'd be damned if she'd let him know it. Like flicking on a light switch, he had suddenly changed from a compassionate man back to the arrogant, egotistical clod she had encountered in the restaurant. "Look here, *Mr.* Garrett!" she snapped. "Just because we're snowbound together and have to make the best of it, don't think we're going to make the best of it, if you know what I mean."

"Aw shucks," he teased. "Don't tell me you're going to be a party pooper."

More outraged than embarrassed by his sauciness, Samantha turned on her side in a huff. Completely forgetting her state of undress, she released the cover, yanked one of the pillows from behind her head, and lunged angrily at the exuberant face beside her. But she wasn't swift enough. Deftly Garrett grabbed the pillow with one hand and raised it high above his head, his laughter deep and throaty.

Samantha automatically leaped up to retrieve the pillow, and her hands collided with his. The pillow dropped like a rock to the floor. Somewhere in the scuffle, she managed to land on top of him. Her milky white breasts ground into his massive furred chest, while her hips fused intimately with his, momentarily stealing the breath from both of them.

A blazing fire ignited in his eyes, and he locked his arms around her. "Mmmmm, that's nice," he purred, a look of pure lust scrawled across his handsome features. Samantha swallowed hard and tried to move away, but he pinned her tightly against him.

"You really don't want me to let you go, do you?" he asked, sliding his hands boldly down the length of her satin-smooth body. When his palms reached her buttocks, she jerked herself up, but he caught the soft flesh in his fingers and pushed her back down against him.

A surge of electricity ran through her, staining her cheeks crimson as she felt his arousal. She tried to fight off the wild excitement the feel of his body had induced. "Take your bloody hands off me!" she choked, turning her head away so that he couldn't see the flame of desire in her eyes. But Garrett did see it, and with the side of his cheek he turned her face to his. "You don't fool me," he taunted. "I can tell you're a wild little sex kitten at heart."

She watched as his gaze traveled to her bare bottom, and she flamed even deeper. Infuriated, she barked, "I am *not* a sex kitten! It's been years–" She caught herself up short at the admission. She hadn't been with a man since her husband died.

"Finish it, Samantha."

"My past is none of your business. Now let me go or I'll–"

"You'll what?" he cut in swiftly. "Scream? I don't think so, because whether you realize it or not, the lower part of your body is grinding against mine without any help from me. Not that I'm complaining, you understand. I love it."

Because I've fallen in love with you, he wanted to say out loud. But he kept still, knowing she'd never believe him. It was hard enough to believe it himself. No woman had ever affected him like this, not even Rosemary...

"I'll just bet you do!" she said tightly.

"And I'll bet the farm that you do, too," he returned, increasing the pressure of his hands.

By now, her heart was pounding so fiercely she thought it would burst from her chest. He was right. Dead right. But she couldn't give in. Somehow she had to find the strength to break away from him before he dissolved all her defenses, or worse yet, before she willingly abandoned them herself. "That's it!" she exclaimed, giving a violent push against his chest. "I'm getting out of this bed. Where else can I get some sleep around here?"

He pointed to a closed door to the left of the hearth. "That's a bedroom, but I'd advise you not to use it."

"Why not?" she asked, grabbing the quilt and pulling it tightly around her.

"Because it's freezing in there."

"Doesn't the room have a stove or a heater?"

"It has a pot belly stove," he answered, "but I'm not going to light it and waste precious wood. On the other hand, if you really want to leave this toasty warm bed, go ahead, be my guest."

Deep down, Samantha really didn't want to go. But she wanted to test him, to see if it mattered one way or another if she stayed or not.

Garrett caught on to her little game and played along accordingly. If she expected him to plead with her to stay, she had another guess coming.

"I could curl up on the captain's chair beside the hearth," she announced, stealing a glance at him.

He simply shrugged his shoulders. "Suit yourself. But there aren't any other blankets, and you can't have this one." She looked him square in the eyes and pouted. "Doesn't seem right that the Whitmans only had one quilt in this place. But if you'd put some clothes on, you could spare me your precious quilt."

"Sorry, my pet," he drawled, giving her a sly little wink. I sleep in the raw, *obuffo*, even in the dead of winter. Now if you're going, go – but do it quietly. I'm going to sleep." With that he pulled the quilt over his shoulder and turned on his side, leaving her to stare at the smooth muscles of his back. Within seconds, his heavy breathing

75

told her sleep had claimed him.

Regardless of the circumstances that had brought her to this cabin, Samantha knew she had no right being in his bed. Even if it meant sleeping in her wet clothes on a hard chair, she knew that's where she should be. And she would have gone quietly as he had ordered, but her heart wouldn't let her. The thought of spending the night next to him brought on a delicious sensual ecstasy – a feeling she hadn't experienced in a long, long time. No, she decided, she wasn't going anywhere. Snuggling deeper under the cover, she dragged her gaze from his back to the glowing hearth, and began remembering the way his hard, strong hands had fondled her curvaceous hips just minutes before. She couldn't deny the provocative sensations he had aroused in her. Neither could she believe the way she had heightened his desire. She had actually seduced him without realizing she was doing it. It was frightening, yet wildly exciting to know she was capable of arousing a man like Tony Garrett.

In her dreamy state, she smiled to herself, feeling wicked and sexy ... until he stirred, and she thought he might wake up and reach out for her in the dark. When he didn't, she frowned. Who was she kidding, she asked herself, and her spirits plummeted. A man like Tony Garrett wasn't so easily seduced. At least not by someone so ordinary as herself.

By this time she had convinced herself that he had been making a fool of her, toying with her, making her think she was a sultry siren, when deep down he must surely loath the sight of her, which explained why he concocted this scheme with Adam to get her here. It was payback time for the unfavorable notoriety and embarrassment she had caused him. Thoroughly depressed now, she turned on her side, gave the pillow a frustrated punch, and went to sleep.

* * * * *

Again, something was making her nose itch. In her half-sleep she surmised it was only the lacing on the quilt, so she twitched her nose deeper into the covering to relieve the tingling sensation. But the more her nose moved in the roughness, the deeper the urge became to sneeze. When the tiny ripple escaped her, her eyes flew open, only to discover her face was flush against his broad, hairy chest. She remained motionless, taking in her unbelievable predicament. His right arm and leg was curled possessively around her, pinning her slender frame to his, while the heady male smell of him seemed so erotic it nearly turned her insides to jelly.

As if on cue, Garrett's eyes slowly opened to meet the contented face of his bed partner.

"Good morning," he murmured sleepily, "I see you reconsidered your options."

"Some options," she said dryly. "A walk-in freezer, a hard chair, and a..."

"Warm inviting bed," he finished, "fully equipped with a warm, inviting man. Now be honest. Who could ask for anything more?"

"Certainly not I," she flipped, sliding her face away. She felt she looked a fright, and it was all she could do to keep from pulling the pillow down on her own face.

"Then why are you turning away from me?" he questioned, stroking her cheek with the side of his hand. When she didn't answer, he guided her face back to meet his smoldering stare. "Am I so revolting in the cold light of

77

day?"

Revolting? Did he actually believe he turned her off? Nothing could have been further from the truth. With his dark, wavy hair tousled about his head, and the remnants of sleep still stamped on his handsome face, he was more seductive than ever.

"Well?"

"Well, what?"

"You didn't answer my question."

She sighed in exasperation. "What do you want, Tony?"

"You," he whispered, pulling her so close and so tight, she could barely breathe. "Now kiss me."

"I-I can't," she protested against her own inner longings. "I won't!"

Garrett wasn't about to take no for an answer. He had ached for this moment since he first laid eyes on her. He had to taste her...feel her...have her...*now*. "Yes, you can," he breathed, "and you will. From this moment on, you'll be begging me to make love t–"

His words were cut off by her soft, warm lips that met his in a wild fusion that took immediate control of both their senses. The force of his mouth opened hers, and he slid his tongue inside. Consumed by the want of her, he crushed her breasts against his chest, barely hearing her soft moans as he probed the inner recesses of her mouth.

For Samantha, it was just too much. Too much wanting ... too much needing ... too much feeling. There was no space in her mind to think, nor could she.

Garrett ravished her with his mouth, keeping his eyes fixed on her, fearing if he closed them, she would vanish.

His mouth still fused to hers, he gently rolled her onto

her back and cupped her soft, tender breast, teasing its tiny pink nipple with his fingers until it too ached to feel his mouth. The hurting but utterly pleasurable sensation of his teeth and tongue on her breast prompted her to move her right hand against his chest and rake the hairs between her fingers.

Lost now in a tidal wave of passion and pleasure, Garrett took her other hand and slowly guided it along the inside of his thigh. When it reached his groin he opened her fingers, then closed them tightly around his throbbing manhood.

The fire in the hearth had flickered and died long ago, while the storm that raged outside slammed with fury against the windows. The room was icy cold, yet streams of sweat covered the about-to-be-lovers. While they were moving to the rhythm of their passion, they had managed to braid the quilt around their legs. Uttering a guttural oath, Garrett grabbed it and flung it to the floor. Without missing a beat, he raised himself high above her and parted her legs with his knees. Ever so slowly, his hand made its way up her thigh until it found its treasure.

Samantha was shivering, not from the cold, but from the exquisite tension his mouth and hands were causing. He cupped her sensitive vee in his hand and fondled her until the tension mounted even higher.

When he felt her moisture in his palm, he slid a finger inside, gently moving it back and forth.

Fireworks exploded in Samantha's head at the intimate invasion.

Garrett began to breathe harder and harder. His control stretched to the limit, he entered her gently, taking care not to hurt her.

Samantha's hips moved in unison with his, meeting his rhythmic motions until she could no longer bear it. They were both on the edge of ecstasy. All she needed was one swift thrust and paradise would be hers.

Garrett took his cue from her. He slid his hands beneath her soft bottom, spreading her thighs even wider. For a split second he drew back, then thrust forward hard and deep.

"Tony!"

* * * * *

He didn't want to break away from her; didn't want to leave the warm softness that held him prisoner inside, but he couldn't ignore the bone-chilling coldness that filled the room. He kissed her softly, slid away to the end of the bed, and grabbed the quilt from the floor. Trying his best to untangle the covers before she caught a cold, Garrett quickly spread it over her, then tucked it deep beneath her shivering body. He quickly climbed into his clothes and then stocked the hearth. While waiting for the flames to become a roaring fire, he turned to her and asked, "What's the condition of Pearce's cabin?"

"It's flooded," she answered. "The pipes burst from the cold, and the water was a good six inches deep when I left. By now, everything must be frozen solid. Poor Adam. Don't you think we should call him?"

Garrett frowned. "No. The storm is still raging. My cell phone won't be able to pick up a signal strong enough to reach him. He's too far away. I'm afraid there's nothing we can do now but wait."

Tears rushed to Samantha's eyes. "I don't want to

wait! I want to go back to the cabin and get my new manuscript. I forgot it on the desk. What if it's ruined? I'll miss my deadline and probably lose the contract as well."

Garrett came to her side. "Maybe so, and maybe not. Either way, you're not going anywhere right now." He gave her legs a gentle pat and went into the kitchen.

While he was gone, her thoughts quickly switched from the catastrophe that had taken place in Adam's cabin to the disaster that had taken place in Garrett's bed just minutes ago. Without thinking, she balled her fists. How could she have been so stupid? Why didn't a bell go off in her brain when he said that from now on she'd be begging him to make love to her? Obviously, it was a classic line that apparently never failed to get a woman into his bed. Unfortunately, she had taken the bait and had fallen for it.

Realistically, there wasn't a chance in hell he meant it – not this powerful man who had women swooning all over him. She squeezed her eyes tight at the fact that he hadn't bothered to use protection. And he had seen to it that she was so caught up in ecstasy that the thought to protect herself never entered her mind. Now what had she gotten herself into? Right then and there, she vowed that what had just happened would never happen again, despite the overwhelming love she felt for him. Sticking to her decision wasn't going to be easy, but she could do it. She *had* to do it.

The kitchen door eased open, and Garrett walked past her, placing two small pans of water on the hearth. After securing them on the logs, he walked to each of the three windows, his groans increasing in volume as he pushed back the heavy finger-tipped drapes. "Good God, the snow drifts must be eight feet high, and there's at least four feet of the stuff on the ground already."

Samantha turned her head away so that Garrett couldn't see the anguish in her eyes. She wanted to scream that this had to be some kind of nightmare. Today was Christmas Eve, and she should be preparing to leave for Tampa instead of being trapped in this cold, primitive cabin with a vain barracuda and his over-active libido. But she held her tongue. No use in resorting to hysterics. It wouldn't get her home any sooner.

A rising flow of steam from the pans brought Garrett back to the hearth. With a potholder he grabbed the handle of one pan and said, "I'm going to wash and shave. The other pan is for you, love."

He called me 'love,' she said to herself. *That's what he probably calls all his women. That way he doesn't have to keep track of their names.*

Once he disappeared into the bath, she hopped out of bed and dressed quickly. When Garrett returned, she rushed past him into the bath. She soon returned to the living room to find Garrett preparing coffee and canned soup over the fire. "Smells delicious," she remarked blandly, suddenly feeling ravenous.

He poured the soup and coffee into large mugs. After handing her hers, he took a seat at the small table in the kitchen. "If I ask you to join me, will you promise not to empty your soup in my lap?"

He was joking, of course, but Samantha didn't appreciate his humor. She wanted to return the insolent remark, but she knew it would spoil her appetite. "You're safe – this time," she declared, glaring across at him. "I'll eat mine here to ensure it." She proceeded to drop one of the cushions from the sofa bed onto the floor before the hearth.

Lowering herself on to it, she crossed her legs yoga-style and ate her soup.

When Garrett finished, he offered her more coffee. "Please," she said stiffly, keeping her eyes glued to the flames. Her chilling attitude told Garrett something was terribly wrong. Thinking she was regretting that they had made love, he asked her point blank, "Are you sorry about what just happened between us?"

Part of her wanted to say no, that it was a dream come true. But when she remembered her vow and the other women she knew were in his life, she quickly answered, "I don't want to discuss it."

"That's not fair," he said, a frown creasing his brow. "I know something's bothering you, and if I've done anything to upset you, I'd like the chance to defend myself."

Samantha wasn't in the mood to listen to another fabrication that slid from his tongue so easily. Besides, at the moment, *he* was not the problem. "It doesn't matter now," she sighed forlornly, taking the cup of hot brew he held out to her. "Seeing that I can't be home with my family this Christmas, nothing matters. Nothing."

"Thanks a lot," he said, feeling he'd been slapped in the face – again. How could she say nothing mattered after what they had just shared? He was in love with her, and unless he had read her wrong, she had just shown him the feeling was mutual. However, now that it was over, she was acting as if she didn't give a damn about him.

The sight of a lone teardrop rolling down her cheek should have touched his heart, instead, it made him furious. "You're not going to cry, are you? Because I hate weepy females."

She slowly turned her gaze from the fire and shot an

83

angry look in his direction. "I just might!" she flared defiantly.

"Temper, temper," he drawled, as he slid another cushion from the bed and dropped it next to hers. When he lowered himself down, he moved dangerously close to her. The heat from his body seared through her thin sweater, and she shuddered. He was so aggressive, so breathtakingly virile. Without wanting to, she remembered glorying in the feel of his hard muscular body, thrilling in the circle of his arms, and touching the heavens when their bodies finally came together.

"Your plans aren't the only ones altered by the storm," he stated, shifting his gaze from her. "I had plans of my own." It was an outright lie, and he knew it. He and Adam had moved mountains to get her here, knowing full well that at least one good blizzard would hit the area during her stay, compelling her to go to him. On the other hand, if it didn't snow, he and Adam had drawn up an alternate plan. But it did snow, and Garrett couldn't have been happier.

Perhaps it was the sorrowful tone of his voice that made Samantha fall for his line. Forgetting his confession of how he and Adam had arranged for them to be together, she reached out to him compassionately. "I'm sorry if I've acted so self-indulgent. It was thoughtless of me. You probably feel worse than I..." Her voice trailed off, and she blinked hard against the tears that brimmed her eyes.

"Don't do that!"

The sudden harsh tone of his voice made her jump.

"I said I hate weepy females!"

Automatically, she spat back vindictively, "Do you hate them as much as you hate mystery writers?"

His mouth pressed into a hard line. "That was a low

84

blow."

"I meant it to be."

An odd look of pain flickered in his eyes. "I know what you're referring to, but you have to understand that I didn't know you at the time."

"I see," she said. "Is that the way you justify it?"

"Justify what?"

"Talking out of both sides of your mouth."

"Listen here," he said. "When the time is right, I'll tell you why I feel the way I do about mystery writers. Until then, I don't want to discuss it!"

"Fine with me," she said, her voice coated with acid. "I'm really not interested. You're an obnoxious, conceited beast, and I'm glad you're alone this Christmas!"

She was goading him, and he loved it. "Oh, but I'm not alone," he murmured softly, as a disquieting glitter in his eyes roamed her angered face. "I have *you*."

Before she knew what was happening, he coiled the strands of her thick auburn hair between his fingers and eased her head back so that her body slid helplessly down on the cushions. His disturbing nearness caused her pulse to hammer furiously in her throat. She didn't want to be captivated by him, but it was useless. His warm breath fanning her cheek was exquisite torture, making her come alive with want for him. "It's not going to happen again!" she cried, refusing to give in to him.

"Yes it is, love. Why are you being so difficult?"

"I'm not being difficult. Can't you take no for an answer?"

"No."

"Ooooooh," she seethed, fed up with the game he was playing. He was taunting her repeatedly, and she was

85

beginning to hate him for it. Directing her narrowed gaze to his, she spat, "Are you so hard pressed to satisfy your lust that you don't care who you sleep with?"

Garrett moved his head back. "Is *that* what you think?" he rasped.

"That's exactly what I think," she replied haughtily. "You've made up your mind to have sex, and because I'm the only female available at the moment, I'm the lucky candidate."

Garrett felt as if he'd been punched in the gut. "You're wrong, Samantha," he muttered fiercely.

"Am I?" she hissed back. "Then prove it by letting me go!"

"You really don't want me to do that."

"Stop telling me what I want and don't want!"

She raised her arm to thwart his dark face just inches away, but he grabbed her by the wrist and pinned her arm to the cushion. Her body, now molded to his, struggled against the love tide of his desire.

"I'd rather battle the blizzard outside than make love to you again!" she choked out, hoping she had delivered the fatal blow to his over-inflated ego.

Garrett impaled her with his spearing gaze, and Samantha knew she had pushed him too far. "That's a lie," he hissed, his mouth twisting in cynical amusement. "Every nerve in your body is responding to me. Fight it all you want, sweetheart, but you've been begging for this to happen again since the first time."

"You're insane!" she cried furiously, while a little voice in the back of her mind told her he spoke the truth.

Laughing softly, he lowered his face and began nibbling lightly on her ear. "I want you, Samantha," he

86

groaned huskily, "not because you're available but because I–"

Samantha stopped his words by jerking her head to the side. Using all her strength, she tried to writhe free from his iron grasp, but he tightened his hold on her wrists and secured her to the cushion with his weight.

"Let go of me!" she protested, fighting now like a lioness. But his body was on hers like a cement block, pressing harder with each move she made. When she could resist no longer, he released her wrist and urged her face to meet his smoldering gaze. "It's no use, love, so stop fighting it."

There was a wicked glint in his eyes, a warning that he was not a man to be reckoned with. He was used to having his own way. After all, he was a king. He ruled the airwaves late at night, sitting on his leather throne, his golden crown, a cruel and biting tongue that had the ability to reduce men of power to blubbering fools. What chance did she have against this multi-faceted, self-proclaimed monarch named Tony Garrett?

Pinned beneath his body of steel, Samantha feared the battle was over. He intended to take her here and now. There was no one to hear her cries of reluctance. No one to save her from this magnificent but ruthless specimen of a man who frightened and excited her at the same time. It was this excitement that frightened her the most.

No matter how hard she protested, she wanted him. She said so with her eyes that turned liquid every time she looked at him. Being the pro that he was, Garrett read her like a book. Without warning, he cupped her chin tightly with his hand and pressed his mouth sensuously over hers.

Rockets spiraled in her head as he increased the

pressure of his lips in a soul-destroying kiss that brought low, throaty moans from her. Utterly helpless, she went limp beneath him. She was drowning in ecstasy, her senses too drugged to stop him.

He rose to his knees, arching her spine so that her head fell back listlessly, barely touching the cushions. Their lips fused hungrily together. He urged her teeth apart and thrust his searing tongue deep inside, sliding and rolling it around hers. Inhaling deeply, he drew the very breath from her lungs. She arched against him, straining to receive his long, languorous kiss, wanting ... praying it would go on forever.

All her defenses were lost to his mastery, and he was a master in the art of making love. Every move was planned and controlled. His caresses boasted his expertise. There was no awkwardness when he moved his hands around her back and lifted her body clear of the cushions, securing her flush against him. She was like a feather in his arms, light and airy and molded to him as if she were a part of his body. When at last he relinquished her mouth from his, she groaned in agony. But it was not over yet. Garrett had just begun.

CHAPTER SIX

Catching the fold of her cowl-neck sweater with his hand, he quickly pulled the soft garment down, ripping it at the seams, exposing her small, full breasts to his heated gaze. He was a tiger out of control, and as crazy as it was, Samantha didn't care. Hot, searing lips covered a milky white mound, sending waves of fire soaring through her veins. Her breath came in short, quick spasms as she heaved her naked breast wildly against his burning lips. When they closed over the sensitive peak, Samantha was lost to the strange sensations that were now controlling her. "*Please*, Tony," she begged, a willing captive of his hungry mouth that seared a trail of feather-like kisses across her breasts.

He hesitated a moment then raised his eyes slowly to her. "Please what, my love?" he murmured, his voice barely above a whisper.

"Please make love to me."

No sooner had the words escaped when he released his hold on her. "Seems to me I told you you'd be begging me to make love to you."

Her senses were still reeling from the feel of his mouth on her breasts, but her mind was clear and sharp. Prepared for his sarcastic remark, she looked him square in the eyes. "For a moment I'd forgotten it. Thanks for the reminder. Now get off me. I've had enough of your game-playing."

"This isn't a game, and you know it," Garret uttered in a strangled voice, aching to relive the night before. "I want you, Samantha, only you. Now, if you still want me, come back into my arms."

Unable to resist him, she slid back into his open embrace. With a motion so smooth, so effortless, he slid her body across the cushions and rolled down her slacks, removing her panties with them. With one hand, he quickly pulled off her sweater and dropped it to the floor. The flames from the hearth cast a golden glow over her naked flesh, driving him insane.

She tried to keep still, but the anticipation of what was to come made her writhe with excitement. After throwing off his sweater, he lowered his head to her belly. With his tongue he blazed a trail along its softness, then dipped twice into her tiny navel before making his way lower, while his fingers unfastened the button on his jeans.

Samantha heard his zipper part and watched spellbound as Garrett shoved both underwear and jeans down and off with one swift motion. When his tongue reached its target, Samantha gasped out loud.

Although he wanted to, Garrett didn't linger there. Instead, he continued down, licking the insides of her thighs.

Every nerve in her body cried out for him to put an end to the delicious torture that was consuming her.

The taste, feel, and want of her body was building to a crescendo, but Garrett held himself in check, waiting ... wanting her to take the initiative.

As if she had read his thoughts, she clasped the sides of his head and guided his face to hers. She kissed him gently at first, then savagely, drawing his tongue deep into her mouth. She heard him grunt as she shifted her hips beneath his, urging him on. She wanted him now, and she brazenly parted her legs to receive him. This time he didn't take her gently, but entered her hard and fast. Samantha shuddered at the impact, then lifted her hips higher to take in his full length.

Garrett groaned aloud as the tortuous ache turned into exquisite pleasure.

Both their bodies took hold of their senses, but Samantha struggled to keep her wits about her. She loved him and, by God, she was going to make him love her back. She promised herself that, from this day on, he would never want another woman but her.

Little did she know that Garrett had already made the commitment. He told her so with every look, every touch, every kiss. The problem was that he couldn't verbalize it. He had said *I love you* to only one woman in his whole life, and it had turned out to be his greatest mistake. This time he'd make damn sure his decision to love again came from his heart and not the contents of his pants. However, he was only human, and the lady lying beneath him satisfied that part of him in a way that Rosemary never could...

"What is it?" Samantha asked in a daze, feeling Garrett slow down his pace. She didn't need to be a mind-reader to know his thoughts had suddenly strayed elsewhere. "What's wrong?"

"Nothing, sweetheart," he answered, pressing his lips into the curve of her neck. "I was afraid I might be hurting you, that's all."

It was a lie and Samantha knew it. But she brushed it aside for now, making a mental note to question him about it when the time was right. "No, you're not hurting me," she said, kissing him gently on his ear. "But I intend to hurt you – big time!"

Whatever she meant by that statement made him want to protect himself by withdrawing and pulling away. Better yet, run away. He knew from past experience, the kind of physical pain she was capable of inflicting upon him. His jaw had burned for a good hour from the slap delivered by her dainty little hand on a night not so long ago. Considering the size of her, it should have felt like a love tap. Instead, he'd felt he'd been struck by a two-by-four. He hadn't been able to move then, and oddly enough, he couldn't move now, not with her manicured nails digging into his buttocks. "Ow!" he howled, then laughed.

Her hips rolled upward then down in circular motions, throwing him into a frenzy. Cupping her face in his hands, he slid his bottom lip along hers. Samantha wanted more, but he continued tantalizing her by biting her lips ever so gently, then inching his way to her breasts where he nibbled on their tender peaks. When his mouth reached her navel, she let him linger there for a moment before she released her grip, then slipped her hands under his buttocks. Still fused to him, she managed to roll him onto his back. Garrett tightened his grip around her waist as they slid off the cushions and landed on the braided rug before the hearth.

Their spell still unbroken, she took his hands and placed them on her hips. Again, he felt her nails. Only this time they were clutching his shoulders.

Off in a world of her own, she gently raised and lowered herself repeatedly on him until she saw pure elation come over his face.

He had never allowed another woman, including his ex-wife, to straddle him. To have done that meant he was relinquishing his control over her, making him putty in her hands.

To hell with control, he thought to himself, glorying in the feel of Samantha above him. In this position, he was able to shove himself in even deeper. To ensure it, he quickly removed her hands from his shoulders and entwined them with his. At this point, he couldn't take much more. He was wild now, coiling tension completely overtaking him. With his hands digging into her hips, he hammered away, pulling her down on top of him. Time stood still as they got caught up in their frenzied rhythm.

Thunder exploded in Samantha's head, stripping her of all inhibitions. "Watch me, Tony! Watch me!" she screamed as she straightened her back. He opened his dazed eyes and looked at her, not knowing what she was about to do. Casting a smoldering look on his handsome face, she smiled down at him, ready to give him the thrill of his life. Every nerve in his body rose to the surface, vibrating uncontrollably as he watched her arch her back, slowly raise her arms, lift her long, thick hair high above her head, and rake her fingers through it. A primal scream broke from Garrett at the sight, and he thrust himself deep inside her one last time.

* * * * *

"No more. No more. You're killing me!" he howled, as his hands fell weightlessly by his side.

Samantha slid away, then stretched out like a cat on top of him, exhausted, yet thoroughly satisfied. Locked in each other's arms, they lay together in silence, trying to catch their breaths. Giggling to herself, Samantha wiggled her way up and rested her face on his chest. "How would you rate *that* one?" she asked, toying with the hairs on his chest.

"About a twelve." he gasped.

93

"Is that all?"

Garrett pushed her hair away from her face. "Isn't that enough? One more minute, and I would have been shaking hands with St. Peter at the golden gate."

Samantha faked a frown. "You mean you're not ready for another round?"

Garrett roared with laughter. "Are you kidding me? Right now I couldn't get it up with a pulley."

"Aw, shucks. Now who's the party pooper?"

"Touché," he said with a chuckle.

The fire in the hearth was beginning to die down, and Garrett felt chilled. "Would you mind reaching over and grabbing the quilt?" he asked. "I'd do it, but I can't move my arms."

Snuggled under the quilt, the exhausted couple sighed contentedly. Garrett was just about to doze off when Samantha began nibbling on his ear.

"I can't, sweetheart," he mumbled, thinking she really did want to make love again. He was mistaken. By right, he should've known she'd want to know what happened earlier during their lovemaking. He had given the lame excuse that he was afraid he was hurting her. Thinking back, even he didn't buy it.

Samantha moved away and propped herself up on her elbow. "I know you can't," she said, "but we need to talk. Don't you agree?"

He knew where she was going with this, but he didn't want to open up to her. Not right now. He wasn't ready. Besides, he wasn't used to having someone fire questions at him. That was *his* job, and if he could help it, he wanted to keep it that way. "No, I don't," he answered, keeping his eyes closed.

"Well, I do," Samantha sighed in exasperation. "I want to know the *real* reason you almost stopped making love to me. And don't give me the same answer. I don't believe it. Call it woman's intuition, but I'm sure you were thinking about another woman. Am I right?"

"Yes," he blurted out, knowing how she'd react to his answer, yet somehow feeling compelled to admit the truth. He knew she'd be livid. Worse yet, hurt beyond repair. After what they had just shared, he was certain he'd never be able to explain his way out of the mess he'd just created. Nevertheless, he had to try. "It's not what you think," he said, rubbing the palm of his hand over his eyes.

"Stuff it!" she seethed, overcome with humiliation. Her mind whirled with the knowledge that she had been right all along. His persistent seduction had been nothing more than a trick, a miserable conniving ploy to make a complete fool of her. What was now tearing her insides apart was that he had succeeded in stripping her of all self-respect, leaving her emotions vulnerably exposed and tormented. If he had hit her, it wouldn't have hurt so much.

"I loathe and detest you – you cad!" she spat viciously, shock giving virulence to her tongue.

"No, you don't," he said confidently, tossing aside the quilt.

Numbly, she watched him get to his feet and pull on his clothes. When he turned to speak, she saw fire blazing in his eyes. "You wanted the truth, and when I told it to you, you blew a gasket. If you'd have let me finish ... oh, what's the use," he grumbled, stomping over to the hearth. Frustrated, he tossed a few logs into the fire. "It's pointless to try to get through to you."

"That's not true!"

"Yes, it is! What do you take me for? A fool? Don't you think I *know* you've come to the conclusion that I've been using you repeatedly to satisfy my lust because the love of my life can't be here to share this cozy little love nest with me?"

She opened her mouth to speak, but he stopped her. "Don't answer that! Just get up!" His voice thundered through the silence in the room. "We have work to do!"

Disregarding his command, she rested her head against the sofa and closed her eyes. Little by little, her anger began to dissipate, and a feeling of confusion took its place. Could she possibly be wrong in thinking that the woman who had drifted into his mind *wasn't* his lover? And if she wasn't, then who...

"Well?" he drawled, peering down at her. "Didn't you hear what I said?"

Samantha stiffened as she curled her fingers around her torn sweater and clutched it to her bosom. "I'm sure everyone in a five mile radius heard what you said. Too bad they can't see what you've done to my sweater!"

Garrett looked at the fragile garment, remembering how he had torn it off her with one swift pull, and he softened. He didn't want to fight with her, crazy little spitfire that she was. He loved her. In time, she'd come to know just how much. It was going to take a miracle to convince her, but he would ... in time.

Still gazing at the sweater, his senses went into overdrive. He could still feel her warm, velvety sheath encompassing him, and he wondered, *God, how could she possibly believe I could even want – let alone be in love with – another woman?*

"Ah, excuse me. What about my sweater?"

"I'd say it belongs with my food-covered suit – in the trash." Gently he took the sweater from her and walked into the kitchen, dropping it into the garbage can. "There," he said with a grin. "You're much lovelier without it, anyhow."

"I agree," she said to his surprise. "Now what am I supposed to wear? My jacket?"

He came back and stood before her. "I wouldn't hear of it. So, with your permission, I'll step into the room where I keep the formal attire and select something more suitable to the lady's preference." He returned in a flash holding out a bright red flannel shirt. "Here ya go. This one has your name on it."

He was being facetious, but she didn't care. Reaching out for it, she grabbed it from his hand. "Turn around," she ordered crisply. "The free show is over."

In the split second it took to remove the quilt and slip into his shirt, Samantha was seized by an overpowering chill. She was far from over the effects of the previous night's bout with the blizzard. As soon as the last button was fastened, she darted for the fire. When she thrust her arms forward for warmth, the sleeves rushed down beyond her fingers, nearly dipping into the flames.

Garrett came quickly to her rescue. "Here, let me help you before you set yourself on fire," he said with a sigh as he rolled the soft material over her slender wrists. "I don't know what I would do with a flaming, flaming redhead!"

She wanted to tell him, then changed her mind. Looking down half-heartedly at the shirt that hung several inches below her knees, she grimaced. "Okay, what's this work we have to do?"

"Stay right here," he ordered, his face now illuminated by a bright smile. "I'll bring it to you." He dashed into the bedroom, leaving Samantha to finish dressing, all the while wondering what sort of work would spark such enthusiasm. She didn't wonder for long. A seven-foot Christmas tree was soon dragged out from the cold, empty bedroom by an excited Tony Garrett.

"Isn't it something?" he asked, setting it down far enough from the hearth, yet close enough so that the room began to take on the image of a Christmas card.

"Yup, it sure is something," she remarked, looking at the size of the blue spruce with suspicion. "What do you plan to do with it? Chop it down for kindling?"

A dark, wavy head appeared between the branches. "No, silly, we're going to decorate it. Isn't that what everyone does on Christmas Eve? Or do the folks down south have those awful artificial pink and white ones with the colored bows and silly little apples on them?"

The mention of home brought immediate tears to her eyes. She imagined everyone would be gathered at her house for the traditional Christmas Eve dinner. Her sisters, Claire and Maria, would bake home-made pies and dozens of cookies decorated with colored icing.

"Stop that!" Garrett's startling words pierced her thoughts. "Forget about home!" he snapped angrily, reading her thoughts. "Now, come here and help me."

Wiping the corner of her eye with her sleeve, she walked to the tree. "What do you want *me* to do?"

"Just stand back and tell me if it's straight." Samantha stepped behind the sofa bed and gave the tree the once over. "Looks good to me."

"Great," he said. "Now, get back here and hold it while I nail it to the stand. Dutifully, she obeyed. When he was done, she excused herself and went into the kitchen to wash her hands. "What will we decorate it with?" she asked, wiping her hands on a paper towel.

"We've got lights," he called out, "and there are plenty of decorations in the closet in the alcove." He returned immediately, his arms laden with strings of lights, tinsel and boxes of ornaments. Setting them down on the sofa, he began to quickly move around the cabin, his excitement clearly evident. He reached for the transistor radio on the mantle and switched it on, turning the dial hastily until the melodious sounds of Christmas filled the cabin.

"Much, much better." He smiled, returning the radio to the mantle. "And now for some brandy."

She watched from the doorway as he took a bottle and two glasses from the cupboard above the sink. "Here," he said, "let's get into the spirit of things." After he had poured them both an ample amount of brandy, they walked back to the sofa. Garrett took a long swallow of the smooth liquid, then began uncovering the boxes. "Aha!" he exclaimed. "There are two boxes of tinsel, some round pink and gold balls, three boxes of this gold garland stuff, and, of course, the lights. We'd better start with those first. I'll get on a chair behind the tree and flip the string of lights around to you. You drape the front, okay?"

"Gotcha," she agreed, and like Garrett, she took a long swallow of the brandy. Immediately, the liquor raced through her veins, making her feel warm and tingly all over. Suddenly, strings of lights were thrust at her from behind the tree. Samantha, with not so steady a gait, was beginning to have difficulty keeping up with him. Her first mistake came when she tried to reach higher than her head, and she became tangled up in the wires.

Cursing under his breath, Garrett jumped down off the

chair and slowly began to untangle her.

It wasn't necessary for him to accuse her of being so clumsy. The frown lines on his forehead said it quite accurately. However, it was pure torture for her to remain motionless while his hands touched her body. Her eyes, filled with desire, gazed upward at his unsuspecting face. His thick, dark brows formed a straight line over eyes that wavered between azure and aquamarine. Fringed with long, thick lashes, they cast shadows on his lean, tanned face. Below his aquiline nose were the most sensuous lips she had ever seen ... ever kissed. Suddenly, she wanted to kiss them again. But by this time, he had finished untying her.

Turning back to the tree, he draped the remaining lights along the bare branches. When he was finished, he poured them both a refill.

Still tingling from the effects of the first, she decided to sip hers slowly. Perching herself on the edge of the sofa, she watched while Garrett gathered up the tinsel and placed a large wad of it in her hand. "Now, this part requires complete concentration and expert coordination," he advised, his eyes lowering to the glow on her cheeks. "It's an art, and I'm quite good at it, so watch carefully."

But Samantha was too intent on gazing at his handsome profile to take note of what he was saying. He placed the tinsel, strand by strand, on each separate branch. It hung in long and even rows.

"Think you can do that without bungling it?" he asked, throwing her a wary look. Eagerly, she snapped to attention. "Absolutely," she assured him. Did he think she was an incompetent child who needed to be given explicit instructions on how to hang tinsel? She could do the job as well as he. But first, she wanted to finish her drink. As soon

100

as the glass was empty, she was ready.

She began by draping the tinsel on the middle branches, taking pains to execute the job with perfection. Feeling far from homesick now, the combination of the brandy and the Christmas carols was getting to her, and she began to hum merrily along with the radio.

When the time came to drape the tinsel above her head, she tried to balance herself on tiptoes, but the clasps on the black boots she was wearing became caught on one another. Like a drowning man, her life passed before her as she lunged forward into the tree, careening it over onto Garrett.

"God dammit, McCall!" he bellowed under the mass of tree and decorations. "You're nothing but a clumsy, butter-fingered female! Get the hell away from me before we kill each other!"

CHAPTER SEVEN

Shattered completely by Garrett's vicious dismissal, Samantha darted for the captain's chair and snatched up her jacket with a determined hand. There was no time to evaluate the sensibility of her next move. Her only thought was to flee the cabin and get as far away from him as possible. Pulling on her jacket, she dashed for the door, stumbling awkwardly over his fur-lined boots blocking her exit. Giving them a swift, angry kick, she sent them tumbling towards the sofa. Foolishly disregarding the blizzard, she pulled open the door, leaving it open as she ran out into the storm.

Ice pellets dug into her burning cheeks like stinging needles, while the frigid, blustering wind matted her hair across her face. Each step she took dumped mounds of snow inside her boots, weighing her down to nearly a standstill. Determined to reach Adam's cabin, Samantha strained every muscle in her body to keep from falling into the mountainous drifts that were everywhere. But maintaining a steady balance became an impossible task. In the end, a brutal gust of wind whipped across her back, careening her helplessly forward into the snow.

From out of nowhere, hard, strong hands pulled her upright. They hurled her around, and Samantha saw Garrett's angry face towering above hers. She tried to pull back, but his strength overpowered her. With little effort, he lifted her up into the circle of his arms.

"Let go of me!" she screamed, trying to twist and hammer herself free from the bands of steel that imprisoned her. But the more she fought, the tighter his grip became. Between the storm and her violent poundings of protest, it seemed to take forever to reach the safety of his cabin.

Inside the warm sanctuary, Garrett took their snow-covered jackets and draped them on a chair close to the fire. Unable to harness the anger that shook within him, he turned and threw a furious look at her. "Why the hell did you run outside?" he shouted viciously.

Exasperated, Samantha snapped back, "Because you ordered me to get the hell away from you, so I did! Better that I put up with the mess in Adam's cabin than to be cruelly insulted by you!"

"I'm sorry that I lost it and yelled at you," he apologized while trying to catch his breath. "I really didn't mean what I said. Nevertheless, it was inexcusable." He raked his wet hair with his fingers, feeling absolutely sick inside. "Actually, it was *my* fault. I shouldn't have given you the brandy on an empty stomach. Again, Samantha, I'm so very, very sorry. I'll take care of that problem right away. But first, take off those wet clothes." He stomped off into the bedroom, slamming the door behind him.

While Samantha was wiping her face with the back of her hand, her inspecting gaze traveled to the tree which was lying completely on its side. Her heart dropped. What a mess, she thought, feeling deeply discouraged. What a rotten, miserable mess this Christmas has turned out to be. In her distress, she was tempted to blurt out the words loudly so Garrett could hear them, but she was so spent from battling him and the storm, that the only sound emitted from her throat was a muffled sob.

She was still standing there, a puddle of water forming at her feet, when Garrett reentered the room. Defiantly,

Samantha turned her back to him.

"Here," he said softly, handing her a towel and a dry flannel shirt. "Take that wet one off and dry your hair. I'd give you a pair of my jeans, but they're taller than you are." He turned his head away so she couldn't see him smile.

Muttering a stiff, almost inaudible thank you, she glanced at him. All the anger and frustration she had felt just moments ago instantly dissolved as her eyes took in his provocative attire. He had changed into tight black corduroy pants and a black, long sleeve shirt that was open to the waist, forming an intoxicating vee from his throat to the waistband of his pants. The thick, dark mat of hair on his chest, exposed fully to her view, brought back sweet memories of that morning when she had awakened with her face snuggled flush against it.

She directed her gaze to the fire, unable to look at him. She couldn't believe that they had fought ... again. She turned her back to him and began unbuttoning her shirt, all the while despising herself for the inconsistencies of her feelings. One moment she hated him and wanted nothing more than to put as much distance between them as possible. The next, longing to be near him, to feel his flesh pounding into hers, to be totally possessed by him. The pull of anxiety within her was torturous.

Garrett, uttering the need for a drink, marched into the kitchen. Samantha, thankful for this bit of privacy, shed her wet shirt and pulled the dry one on. When she had freed herself of the sopping wet boots, slacks and panties, she dragged the quilt from the sofa and wrapped it around her middle. After spreading her clothes across the other chair to dry, she sat down on the braided rug before the fire.

She was vigorously rubbing her hair with the towel

when Garrett returned holding two half-filled snifters of brandy. "Drink this before you catch pneumonia," he ordered sharply, "although I'd say you've had more than enough liquor already."

Samantha chose not to respond, much as she would have liked to. Instead, she rested her head back against the sofa and watched Garrett struggle to set the tree upright. When he finished the task, he bent down to her and said, "How does a nice juicy steak sound to you?"

"Swell," she answered flatly. Her stomach growled in agreement.

"And a salad?"

"Fine." He was bending over backwards to please her. He must be feeling awful, she thought to herself, sipping at her brandy. Good, she decided. He deserved to be brought down a peg or two.

* * * * *

Samantha remembered someone once told her that if she ever wanted to get something from a man, she should make him feel guilty, because guilt also made one vulnerable. Samantha had never thought to use that advice until she watched Garrett practically doing cartwheels to make amends. He was bustling around the kitchen, whipping up the salad while Samantha planned her course of action.

It wasn't long before Garrett came into the room, awkwardly trying to balance two trays loaded with food on his arms. One hand struggled with a huge cast iron frying pan, which apparently weighed a ton. "God, that's heavy," he stated, dropping the pan onto the floor. He cast her a helpless look. If he was expecting her to help him, he was dead wrong. She merely gave him a smile and continued to watch him knock himself out.

"Be back in a flash with the steaks."

Before she knew it, he had placed Delmonico steaks in the pan, then set it on the fire. "I like mine rare," he said. "How about you?" Samantha simply nodded. Within minutes, they were both digging into their meals.

Samantha couldn't down hers fast enough. When she placed her fork on the empty dish, she belched, then flamed. "Excuse me," she said, embarrassed. "Guess I was hungrier than I thought."

"I'll take that as a compliment," he replied. "I'm no cook. In fact, I hate cooking."

She lifted her brandy to her lips. Just before she took a sip, she asked coyly, "Do you hate cooking as much as you hate boring mystery writers?"

Garrett almost choked on the piece of steak he was chewing. "You never give up, do you? When are you going to get the message that my feelings about mystery writers is a private thing with me?"

"And you never discuss private things with anyone."

"That's right."

"And that includes me?" she asked. "Are you afraid I might betray your privacy and blab it all over town? Is that the kind of person you think I am?"

Garrett took a gulp of his brandy. "I know from experience that you're pretty outspoken," he answered. "But no, I don't think you'd reveal anything that's discussed here tonight. In fact, I'd probably feel relieved to finally get it off my chest once and for all."

Samantha backed away a little at the admission, but

Garrett pulled her back. "If you want to know the whole story, sweetheart, don't stop me now." Samantha felt a stab at her heart, but she let him go on.

He spoke in a tone that was almost menacing. "It began with Rosemary Delahunt!"

"Who's Rosemary Delahunt?"

"She was an English professor who tutored me in creative writing. I was a rookie news reporter for a cable television station in Portland, Oregon. She knew I devoured mystery novels, and that my dream was to one day write a best seller. We met twice a week at my place to ensure privacy from my colleagues. I didn't want anyone to know, just in case it didn't work out. As far as a teacher goes, she was brutal. Nothing I ever wrote pleased her. She ended up calling *me* a no-talent, boring, hack writer, and that I should stick to reporting the news. I was devastated.

Two years later, we ran into each other in New York City. She looked so different, I hardly recognized her. She was absolutely gorgeous. I fell head over heels in love with her. She chased after me like a bitch in heat, winding herself around me like a snake, wanting me to make love to her every chance we got. By this time, she had become one of the nation's hottest mystery writers. Every book made the *New York Times* best seller list. And she refused to write under her given name. So, like you, she chose a man's name.

Anyway, one night we were having dinner at a place called Broadway Joe. It's a steak house over on West Forty-Sixth Street. It's also a sports and celebrity hangout. I'd been anchoring the eleven o'clock news for about a year, so just about everyone in the place knew who I was.

During the meal I told Rosemary I loved her, and I

107

asked her to marry me. She jumped at the proposal. Two weeks later, we were married. The press played it down, simply stating I had married a non-celebrity. Rosemary insisted her true identity be kept a well-guarded secret. Right then and there I should've suspected that something was wrong.

My troubles began during our honeymoon in Monaco. She kept refusing to make love with me, using the lame excuse that she was uptight because she had a deadline to meet, and she wanted to return to New York to finish her book. She was so insistent, it was fruitless to argue with her, so we came home. Well, one day I was in my office preparing for the news, when I suddenly became ill. I'd caught the flu, so the station got a replacement for the telecast and I went home early. When I entered my apartment I got the shock of my life. There was my wife in bed with another man."

Shocked at the admission, Samantha pulled away from him. "You can't be serious!"

"Of course I'm serious," he replied. "I'm also ticked off at myself for being so stupid for not having her investigated *before* we got married."

"Did you know who the man was?"

"Unfortunately, yes. He's one of New York's most controversial figures. *And* he's a married man. I filed for divorce immediately, claiming irreconcilable differences. I just wanted out without causing a scandal. I couldn't take the chance of damaging the career I'd worked so hard to achieve."

Samantha's head reeled at the revelation. Garrett continued. "I didn't know it was *you* behind the curtain the night we first met. Louie knows how much I detest mystery writers, but he still doesn't know why. You and my attorney are the only ones who do. Now do you understand why *I* call mystery writers boring?"

"Well, now I do, although I don't think it's fair. And I find it strange that after all this time, you haven't been able to let it go. All us mystery writers are not like her."

He reached out to her and wrapped his arms around her so tightly, she could barely breathe, yet she somehow knew the story wasn't over yet. She inched her face away and looked into his eyes. They were brimming with tears.

"Tony, what's wrong?"

Garrett sucked in a deep breath to regain his composure. "She was the only woman I ever said *I love you* to. I've never been able to say it since ... never allowed myself to get close enough to a woman to become that vulnerable until–" He wanted to say *now*. But he still couldn't. Instead, he stopped and took a firm grip of her hands.

"This morning, when we were making love, I had a flashback of my wedding night. Rosemary and I were ... well, you know. I can't remember why I opened my eyes during it, but I did. What I saw sickened me. Instead of watching the face of my bride smiling contentedly, I saw her head turn away, as if she couldn't wait to get it over with. That's what I was thinking when I slowed down my pace. I didn't even realize I was doing it." He buried his face in the curve of her neck. "I'm sorry, sweetheart. I didn't want you to think that I was wishing I was making love to someone else. As God is my witness, I've never, *never* experienced such ecstasy in my life as I have with you."

Exhausted but relieved that it was finally all out in the open, he released her hands, looked up at her somber face, and gave her a long, soulful kiss. Samantha wanted more, and so did Garrett, but he pulled himself away and rose to his feet. With a broad smile he announced, "It's Christmas Eve, my love, and Santa Claus braved the blizzard to see that you got your presents."

What presents? she asked herself, watching him gather up the dirty dishes and take them into the kitchen. She was glad to be alone for a minute or two so that she could digest all that had happened in the last few hours. After disclosing the horrors of his past marriage, which was enough to turn any man away from taking a second plunge, she began to understand his determination to keep his life private. However, without saying it outright, he had made the point that he would never allow himself to fall in love again. So, her provocative demonstration of being the ultimate sex kitten had failed.

Remembering back, she had vowed to make him want her to the point where he'd never want another woman again. By the way they'd made love repeatedly, she'd thought she had succeeded. Apparently, she was wrong. Never one to accept defeat graciously, she decided her quest was not over. She would use all her feminine charms to locate that vulnerable spot in his heart, then capture it ... tonight.

She was smoothing her rumpled hair with her fingers when Garrett re-entered the room.

"How does Dom Perignon sound for starters?" he asked, placing the bottle and two glasses before her on the floor.

"Wonderful," she answered, feeling confident the champagne wouldn't affect her, now that her stomach was full. Eyes wide with wonderment, she watched him enter the bedroom. When he came out, he was holding two packages. Both were beautifully wrapped in green embossed paper, topped off with gold satin bows. Garrett gently set them down on her lap. Grinning like the cat who ate the canary, he darted into the alcove and returned with four red candles. After placing them in glass holders, he lit them and set two on the mantle, and the others on the end tables that flanked the sofa bed. Between the flickering flames in the hearth, and the glow from the lighted candles, the room was transformed into a romantic Christmas paradise.

At sometime during his bustling about, Garrett had turned on the radio, lowering the volume so that the melodious sounds of violins playing Christmas carols could be heard softly in the background. He curled up beside her on the rug and opened the bottle of champagne, taking pains to keep the bubbles from spilling over. When the glasses were filled, Garrett gently tapped his glass against hers. "Merry Christmas, Samantha," he said, as he leaned over and placed the lightest, softest kiss on her lips. Samantha's heart skipped a beat as their lips touched. "Merry Christmas, Tony."

After swallowing an ample amount of champagne, he said, "When I was a little boy, my grandmother told me that everyone was supposed to make a wish on Christmas Eve, and that the Christmas angel on the top of the tree would grant it. Make a wish, Samantha."

For a moment, Samantha couldn't think; couldn't move. Like a child experiencing Christmas for the first time, she looked around the room in wide-eyed wonder. He had gone to great lengths to keep her mind off her home and family, and he had succeeded. His diligent efforts had touched her heart, and she fought back tears of joy as she took a sip of champagne, then lifted her eyes to the satin angel atop the tree and made a wish.

"Care to tell me what it was?" he asked coyly.

"Nope." she teased, "because if I do, it won't come true." Lord knows how she wanted to tell him, but she was afraid that if she did, it would spoil everything.

"Then open your gifts."

Samantha's heart dropped as she looked down at the presents on her lap. "I can't accept these, Tony. Besides, I feel awful. I don't have a present for you."

Yes you do, he wanted to say, but didn't dare. Her love was the best Christmas present a man could want, for it was the gift that made every day Christmas. "Just your being here to share this holiday with me is more than enough. Now, open them."

"Gimme a hint," she prompted.

Garrett chuckled and shook his head. "Sorry, no hints. Just open them. I can't wait to see the expression on your face when you see them."

"Here goes," she said, after taking a long swallow of champagne, hoping it would steady her shaking hands. She unwrapped the smaller gift and removed the cover from a tiny white box.

"Tony!" she exclaimed, feasting her eyes on the most beautiful pink and white cameo brooch she had ever seen. "My God, this is gorgeous! It must be an antique."

"Yes, it is," he answered, his bright blue eyes shining with pride. "It was my grandmother's. My grandfather gave it to her on their wedding day."

"I gather this is the same grandmother who told you about making a Christmas wish," she teased.

"That's the one. Now, hurry and open up the other

one."

Why he was in such a hurry to have her see it eluded Samantha, so instead of removing the wrapping slowly, she practically tore it in shreds. What she saw made her shake her head in confusion. "I don't understand, Tony. It's a copy of my book."

"Flip back the cover," he said. She obeyed without question. Scrawled on the inside cover were the words, Best Wishes, Sam McCall.

She looked across at him, her mouth opened in shock. "Where did you get this?"

"At Barnes and Noble, where else?"

She took another gulp of her drink. "You mean you were there? Why? How come I didn't see you?"

"Slow down," he said, laughing. "I went there to see you again. I tried calling your hotel room after the broadcast, but no one answered the phone."

"You mean that was *you* calling?" she asked, astonished. "I was there, but I was afraid it was someone on your staff who was about to threaten me with a lawsuit! Is that why you came to the book store? To threaten me? And how ... how did you get through that mob without being spotted?"

"I disguised myself. Did a damn good job, too. Nobody recognized me. Not even you. And no, I didn't go there to threaten you. I was hoping the crowd would leave before I did so that I could apologize for my rudeness. I really was sorry, and I still am. Will you ever forgive me?"

She wanted to take him in her arms and squeeze the daylights out of him. "Of course I forgive you. Will you forgive me for dumping the food on you at the restaurant?"

"No, my pet," he answered in jest. "I'll never forgive

you for ruining my brand new suit."

"Then I'll show you what a good sport I am and buy you another one. Now, may I please have some more champagne?"

Garrett gave them both a refill. He should have kept a keener eye on her. He no sooner put the bottle down, and she asked for more. "That's it, sweetheart, you've had your quota for the night."

Samantha gave him her famous pout. "I'm not drunk. I swear it. I just feel warm and cozy all over." *And horny*, she said to herself. "Don't spoil this beautiful night, Tony. It's Christmas Eve. I'm on the floor. How much trouble can I get into here?"

"Talk about a loaded question!" He laughed as he filled their glasses again.

This time she sipped her drink, but it was too late. The champagne had taken over. Ever so slowly, she lifted her hand and slid it inside his open shirt. Garrett shuddered at her touch. "You're playing with fire," he breathed.

"I know I am," she answered, pressing her moist lips to his throat.

"Tell me how much you want me," he whispered, moving her lips from his throat. "Tell me again and again. I need to hear it."

"You know how much I want you, Tony. I've told you so, over and over again."

The champagne that had rushed to her head, now rushed to his. With one swift movement, he threw the quilt off her, exposing her naked body to his view. Eyes blazing with desire, he looked at her as if he were seeing her naked for the first time. Scanning her legs, thighs, and the fine auburn hair that covered her entry into heaven, he uttered in a low throaty voice, "Undress me, and hurry." Heavy need for her was throbbing in his loins.

The last time they had made love, she took the initiative, and he'd loved it. He wanted her to do it again. Only this time he wanted her to start at the beginning ... by stripping off *his* clothes. The shirt was easy. Only one button held it together. With both hands she pulled the garment out of his pants, unfastening the button with the force of it. Two seconds later, it lay on the floor. To undo his pants, they both got to their knees. Smiling wickedly, Samantha undid the snap. His zipper parted with ease, exposing his erect, pulsating member. Samantha thrilled repeatedly at the sight. He wore no underwear, so his pants slid easily down his thighs. He leaned against the sofa just as she got to his knees, and with one swift yank, his pants and socks joined his shirt.

They were both on their knees again, mouths fused together, while their hands roamed each other's body. When his lips left hers and went to her breasts, she threw back her head. "More, Tony, more," she moaned while she took both his hands and placed them on her breasts. Her chest heaved wildly as he played with her nipples. Wild shivers raced through her. She grabbed his buttocks and ground his arousal against her. It was so erotic, and she knew neither of them would be able to stand it much longer.

Easing Samantha down onto the rug, Garrett lay on his back and pulled her on top of him. He parted her legs and thrust himself inside, jutting his hips against hers in a wild frenzy.

He cupped her buttocks hard, making sure she'd meet him thrust for thrust. "Look at me and tell me how much you want *me*," she ordered harshly. "Tell me, then show

115

me!"

"Good God, babe, I want you with all my heart," he groaned, washed up in the same tidal wave that was rushing through her. "Now I'm going to show you!"

Sliding his arms of steel under her thighs, he raised her legs and draped them over his shoulders. Then returning his hands to her bottom, he pulled himself up, keeping himself locked deep inside her. "How's this?" he asked, rocking her back and forth. She didn't answer. She didn't have to. The glazed look in her eyes said it all. He captured her mouth with his, drawing the very breath from her.

She could feel the explosion coming, and she tried to stop it by shifting her mind elsewhere, but she couldn't. Wave after wave shuddered through her, causing her to scream at the intensity of it.

Garrett heard her cry out, and his excitement soared as spasms ripped through him.

When Garrett forced himself even deeper inside her, Samantha felt a new surge of ecstasy, the second time more powerful than the first. The combination of the champagne and the multiple explosions were more than she could take. She couldn't see ... couldn't control any part of her body ... couldn't keep from losing consciousness...

CHAPTER EIGHT

When Samantha finally came to, she slowly opened her eyes and saw she was no longer on the floor, but on the sofa. She could feel his body flush against her, scorching her with its furnace-like heat. It sparked to life the familiar wanton, aching need for him, while at the same time producing deep feelings of guilt and shame over her promiscuous behavior the previous night.

She shut her eyes in self-condemnation, but was soon jolted from her penitence by a sudden vibration that shook the entire cabin. It startled her so much that she drew Garrett even closer to her.

"My God, Tony! It's an avalanche! We're going to be buried alive!"

Caressing her gently, Garrett nuzzled his chin in her hair. "It's not an avalanche, sexy." he reassured with a chuckle. "It's just the heavy snow sliding off the roof and hitting the ground. Relax. In a few minutes everything will be back to normal."

Back to normal. He had to be joking. Since the moment this man had entered her life, Samantha's world had been turned upside down, guaranteeing it would never be normal again.

A slow, lazy smile played on his lips. "You were *wonderful* last night."

Samantha cringed, not only at the implication, but at the memory of her loose behavior. Humiliated, she dragged herself free from his embrace and rolled over onto her stomach, too ashamed to look at him.

117

"I was anything but wonderful," she spat angrily. "I drank too much, I-I threw myself at you like a street-walking harlot, then passed out cold." She felt tears rush to her eyes. "I'm so ashamed, I could die!"

The regrettable tone in her voice was not lost to Garrett, who urged her onto her back so that she was forced to look at him. His gaze was warm and sympathetic, which made Samantha feel even worse.

Why is he torturing me this way? she agonized. He doesn't love me, or he would have told me by now, so why doesn't he just leave me alone? But Garrett was not to be put off. When she shut her eyes to avoid his piercing gaze, he commanded harshly, "Open your eyes and look at me! Her cheeks flamed as she raised her long, sweeping lashes.

"That's much better," he said, caressing her cheek with feather-like strokes. "I said you were wonderful last night because I meant it. Is that so shameful?"

"Yes," she muttered. "It wouldn't have happened if I hadn't insisted on that last glass of champagne. It went right to my head, and I lost it."

He lowered his dark head, stopping inches from her parted lips. "You didn't lose it, honey, you merely set yourself free, and so did I. Stop making excuses. What happened last night happened because we both wanted it to." His lips were so close that their breaths mingled, and Samantha knew it was impossible to argue the fact.

"Okay, you're right," she whispered, a mixture of excitement and confusion churning inside her. "I did want it to happen, but—"

He stopped her explanation by covering her mouth with a soft, tender kiss. Kissing him back, she felt her lower limbs go weak as his hand began to wander down below her waist. His breathing became labored, and she knew he wanted to make love again. So did she, but this time she pulled the reins on her emotions.

"Stop, Tony ... please..." she begged, pushing his hand away. "This can't go on any longer. I'm not liberated enough to walk away from this affair unscarred. But you, you're different. You're a celebrity, and celebrities are notorious for their casual affairs. Well, I'm not going to let myself be one of your assembly-line lovers. You're not going to use me, then cast me aside like yesterday's newspaper."

"Are you through?" he rasped. Without waiting for her answer, he continued,. "Believe it or not, I don't bed down every female who crosses my path. If I did, I'd be in a jar in the Smithsonian Institute. But I'm not a candidate for sainthood, either. I admit to having my share of women. But I wish you wouldn't be so quick to judge me and assume I'm some kind of sex fiend. Regardless of what you think, I'm not a love 'em and leave 'em kind of guy. Frankly, it disturbs me to think you actually believe I consider you nothing but a conquest!"

Samantha managed a calm but stiff reply. "What else am I supposed to believe? You shower me with all the pickings of a romantic little interlude, like a fabulous meal, a cozy fire, and your grandmother's beautiful pin. Then to guarantee a successful seduction, you produce a bottle of Dom Perignon. I didn't have a snowball's chance in hell. So now, here I am, lying naked in your bed, *again*, and you can't understand why I feel I'm nothing other than one more conquest."

She clutched the quilt around her and slid over to the opposite side of the sofa, her decision made. She had to get away from him...*now*! The question she refused to confront was, who was she running from – Garrett or herself?

She turned her back to him and got up unsteadily. "Whether the storm is over or not, I've just got to get out of here, Tony. I can't handle this anymore."

"You're not leaving me again!" Garrett roared, and with one swift hand he swung her around and caught her in his arms. His eyes bore deeply into hers. "Don't you *ever* turn away from me," he taunted, arching her back so that their bodies were fused tightly together.

Samantha's eyes lowered to her breasts embedded deeply into his chest. She swallowed hard, feeling more aroused than frightened. He glared down at her, his eyes wild and fiery. "Look me straight in the eyes and tell me I mean nothing to you!"

Samantha twisted her face in agony. "What do you care how I feel about you? Not once have you told me that your interest in me is anything but purely physical." She closed her eyes against the hurt she didn't want him to see, yet the pain was clearly evident in her quivering voice. "You've accomplished your mission, so what more do you want from me?"

"I'll tell you what I want," he groaned huskily against her cheek, "I want you to marry me... today."

Samantha's eyes rounded, and her mouth opened in shock. "What did you say?" She was certain she had heard wrong.

"I said, I want to marry you today."

"Is this your idea of a joke?" Before he could answer, she was on him again. "Did anyone ever tell you that you have an *I* problem? Because all I've heard since I got here is, *I* want this, and *I* want that!"

His arms flexed into bands of steel as he pushed her away and then bolted upright into a sitting position. He moved so fast that he dragged the quilt with him, causing her to lie there naked to her knees. She automatically lunged down to grab the cover, only to have Garrett thwart her efforts by grasping her wrist.

"Cut it out!" she demanded. "I'm freezing!"

"Good," he snapped. "Maybe you'll cool off long enough to listen to reason." His blue eyes glinted with anger as he turned to face her. "Believe me, sweetheart, if getting you into my bed was my only priority, it would've happened long before you came to the mountains. I've never had to propose marriage to get what so many women are all too eager to give away. And you, my dear, were eager."

To Samantha, his flippant remark was like pouring salt on an open wound, a wound she had created herself. Since they'd first made love, she'd been hell-bent on worming her way into his heart so that he'd never want another woman but her again. And she'd accomplished her mission. But never in her wildest imagination did she expect her quest to result in a marriage proposal.

Talk about stacking the deck in her favor! Having been married before, she knew what men loved, what made them go wild. All she had to do was take the initiative and fulfill his fantasies. She knew how to taunt and seduce Garrett; stimulate him to the point where sanity became overruled by undulating excitement; excitement he had never experienced with anyone ... including his ex, Rosemary.

Pulling her wrist free, Samantha covered herself with the quilt, and waited in silence for him to finish.

"When you stormed out on stage that night, you did

more than slap me. You captivated me. Despite your over-zealous attempt to put me in my place, you looked so tiny and fragile, I wanted to sweep you up into my arms and cradle you like a woman-child. Right then and there, I decided that you were the one for me. That's why I'm asking you to marry me." He paused to touch her cheek. "I love you, sweetheart. I knew it then, and even though you've tried to maim me three times, I'm sure of it now. So, get it out of your head that what we've been sharing all along was nothing but sex. We've been making love, Samantha, like nobody's ever made love before."

Still dazed from his proposal, she shook her head and queried, "How can you ask me to make a lifelong commitment to you? We're barely more than strangers. You know nothing about me."

Garrett's mouth curled into a smile. "Really? Then correct me if I'm wrong. You were born almost thirty-one years ago in Buffalo, New York, the daughter of a police captain now retired, who is plagued with a severe case of arthritis, which is why your family retreats to Tampa every winter. You were married to a state trooper named Frank Maguire for only four months before he was killed on the job in a tragic accident. You resumed your maiden name after his death and quit your job as a court stenographer to devote yourself to full-time writing."

His smile broadened. "How's that for beginners? I even know you kissed your first boyfriend on your twelfth birthday. His name was Tommy Grant, and that momentous occasion happened behind a billboard next to the railroad tracks. Your own parents don't know about Tommy, but I do."

Samantha was horrified. "How do you know all this?"

122

The smile faded from his lips, and he slid his hand from her cheek. "It's my business to know these deep, dark secrets. That's what sets me apart from all the rest. Where the others tend to stress people's accomplishments and stroke their talented feathers, my staff probes among the cobwebs and digs up not only the treasures, but also the skeletons. And it's *that* information I use if I choose to, and ninety-nine percent of the time, I choose to."

Infuriated to the bone, Samantha fired back. "You're despicable! How dare you have me investigated! My private life, past and present, is none of your business! What gives you the right to infringe on my privacy?" Her nerves were at a screaming pitch.

Garrett studied her angry face for a long moment before he stated tautly, "I had to do it, Samantha. I had to protect myself. What if you were still married, or carrying on an illicit love affair the way my wife was doing? I'd look like a prize fool proposing marriage to you. Not only that, I have to consider my status in relation to the media. They don't care if I have lady friends, nor do they care that I'm divorced. But if I'm going to get up on stage before millions of people every night and hit them where they live, then I'd better be as pure as the driven snow. I can't be afraid that someone will come back with evidence that could ruin me.

"For God's sake, look what happened to me on stage the night we met. There was no time to do my homework on you. I didn't even know you were a woman. After that, the press had a field day with us, and all I did was do my job."

Oh, he did his job, all right! Samantha suddenly felt like a specimen under a microscope. Yet, as much as she hated to, she had to admit he had a valid point. A man in his position couldn't afford to take foolish chances or make mistakes.

"So, what do you say?" he asked, interrupting her thoughts.

"About what?"

"About marrying this thirty-seven-year-old-guy who happens to be crazy in love with you, *that's what!*"

"Why does it have to be today?" she asked, her mind in a whirl. "It's Christmas. Not only that, we've just had a blizzard. Everything must be shut down. And ... and what are our chances of finding someone who *can* perform the ceremony?" She paused and took a deep breath. "I-I don't know, Tony. Why can't it wait until we get back to New York City, and do it the right way? What's the rush?"

"I'll tell you what the rush is. You see how we are right now?" he asked, spreading baby kisses over her face and neck. "This is the way I want to spend the rest of my life, starting today – Christmas Day. I want you beneath me every night, and beside me every morning. I want to open my eyes and look at your beautiful face that radiates with love for *me* and only me. Now it's your turn to tell me that you love me ... that is, if you *do* love me!"

There was no point in denying it; no reason to keep the love she had for him locked up inside any longer. "Yes, you crazy tall person," she joked, covering his throat with kisses. I know it's insane, but I do love you."

"And you want to become Mrs. Anthony Paul Garrett today?"

"Yes, Santa," she giggled, turning to look at the angel atop the tree. Giving the religious ornament a wink, she whispered, "Thanks for making my Christmas wish come true."

"Good!" he exclaimed, giving her bottom a love tap.

Then let's get this show on the road!" With lightening speed he hopped off the sofa, threw some logs on the fire, and jumped into his clothes.

Samantha brought her knees up to her chest and watched excitedly as Garrett darted around the room.

He went to one of the windows and pushed back the drapes. The snow was so high, it covered half the window, but Garrett couldn't have cared less. It was Christmas morning. The storm was finally over, and huddled in his bed was his beautiful bride-to-be.

CHAPTER NINE

"No way!" Samantha balked when Garrett insisted she wear the ugly black boots over her shoes. "I refuse to be seen in public in these hideous things!"

"You'll wear them and like it," he stated coldly. The dark look in his eyes warned Samantha he wouldn't budge an inch until she put them on.

"Good," he said, when she finished. "Without those, your dainty little feet will be frostbitten by the time we reach the village."

"What's in the village?" she snapped, fastening the clasps.

"Anything and everything your little heart desires," he answered. "Hunter Mountain is one of the largest resort areas in upper New York State. People from all over the country come here to ski in the winter, especially at Christmas time. It's fabulous. There are clothing stores, jewelry shops, fine restaurants and quaint little diners and inns. But the best part is that there are a slew of clinics," He took a set of keys from his jacket pocket. "We'll have our blood tests taken, and if luck is with us, someone will know where we can get a license and even a minister."

"And I thought *I* was the one who lived in Fantasy Land," she quipped, slipping into her jacket.

When she was ready, Garrett pulled a red, white, and blue stocking hat onto her head. It was so big, it kept slipping down over her eyes. She looked so comical, he wanted to laugh, but didn't dare.

She, on the other hand, wanted to kill him.

Together they trudged around the cabin to a large wooden shed, where the kindling, Garrett's Hummer, and a snowmobile were kept. Standing there with watery eyes and teeth chattering from the cold, Samantha waited patiently while he cleared a pathway to the door, then guided the snowmobile out onto a narrow roadway. Seconds later, she sat straddled on the black leather seat behind him. They had gone about two hundred yards when Samantha decided she despised the bright yellow vehicle.

Like a motorcycle on skis, it traveled so fast that, in order to maintain her balance, Samantha was forced to clasp her arms tightly around Garrett's waist. Furthermore, the narrow blades kept slicing into the snow banks, causing ice pellets to slam into her face while the gale winds continued to push the stocking cap down over her eyes. Ultimately, she couldn't see the picturesque beauty that surrounded her. Not that she cared. All she could think about was her frightful appearance. Getting married in a wrinkled pants suit, old rubber boots and flat frizzy hair was a far cry from the Grecian curls, satin gown and finger-tipped veil of her dreams.

She had always imagined herself being driven to a cathedral-like church in a sleek white limousine with a dozen bridesmaids and ushers in attendance. She could hear the ooohs and aaahs wafting from the guests as she waltzed down the aisle to the waiting arms of her handsome groom, while a soloist sang the traditional wedding song, *O Promise Me*. It had been such a lovely dream. She couldn't help but give a rueful sigh to think that a short yellow snowmobile was replacing the sleek limousine, and the cathedral-like church would probably be a drafty log cabin. The pants suit, stocking hat, and boots she didn't want to think about.

Before long, Garrett brought the snowmobile to a stop before a red and white brick emergency facility. Once inside, he walked around the corner to the reception desk while Samantha stayed behind, fumbling in her purse for a comb and mirror. After producing both, she sat down on a nearby bench, removed her hat, and smoothed her hair back to its original style.

Because the facility had no holiday casualties to delay them, they were tended to immediately by a young male technician who ushered them into a small, sterile-like cubicle. Seated side by side, Samantha and Garrett smiled at one another while the technician drew a small vile of blood from each of them.

When the tests were completed, Samantha rose quickly to her feet, only to have the room spin like a top around her. Quick to notice she was about to faint, Garrett circled her waist with his arm. She thankfully leaned against him for support.

"You're lightheaded because we had nothing for breakfast but coffee," he reminded her. "As soon as we get the report, I'll take you across the street to the coffee shop."

The thought of food brought a sigh of relief and an immediate smile to Samantha's lips.

No sooner did they walk into the crowded cafe and seated themselves down in a corner booth, when a group of squealing young females flocked to their table, pleading for Garrett's autograph.

"Happens all the time," he whispered, winking at Samantha, who groaned inwardly as she encountered their ecstatic faces. Picturing herself lying prone on the floor, having a hypoglycemic attack, Samantha willed them away.

When they finally left, Garrett ordered coffee and doughnuts from a chubby teenage waitress, who all but drooled over Garrett. She didn't seem to notice Samantha, which was fine, because by now, his bride-to-be was beginning to turn a sick shade of green. Before her complexion resumed its natural pink flush, Samantha devoured three honey-dipped doughnuts and two cups of steaming black coffee.

"Feeling better now?" Garrett asked, finishing his drink. "Much," she replied, dabbing at the corners of her mouth with her napkin.

"Good," he answered. "Now you wait here. I'm going into the kitchen to speak to the manager. I'll bet he knows where we can find someone to marry us."

When he came back to the table, Garrett was smiling from ear to ear. "We're in luck," he said. "There's a judge who lives off the road from our cabin. There's also a lovely boutique further up this road. You can buy yourself a new wardrobe if you like. Next door to it is a jewelry store where you can pick out the wedding ring of your choice. And, last, but not least, the town hall is open. We can get a license there. I just know that nothing can possibly go wrong on our wedding day."

Arm in arm, they made their way out the door, laughing gaily in the midst of the gawking stares and gossiping lips of the crowd they left behind.

* * * * *

An hour and a half later, they were on their way to get married. At the boutique, Samantha bought a brown fur hat that matched her jacket, and a pair of brown leather high heeled boots. She was just about to put them on, when she

129

decided against it. As ridiculous as it was, she suddenly wanted to wear Adam's boots, calling them her *good luck charms*.

The jewelry store was mobbed with people purchasing last-minute Christmas gifts. Garrett headed in the direction of the display case where row upon row of diamond engagement and wedding bands were displayed. He turned around, expecting Samantha to be behind him, but she had wandered off to the area where the plain gold wedding bands were located.

"Wouldn't you like a diamond wedding set?" Garrett asked, stepping to her side.

"I'm not a razzle-dazzle kind of person, Tony," she replied. "I'd be happy with a plain gold band. How about you? Or, perhaps you don't want to wear one."

Garrett gave her a squeeze. "Of course I want to wear one," he said. Samantha smiled back sheepishly. "If it's okay with you," she remarked, "I'd like to buy you your ring. Call it my Christmas present to you."

Garrett balked at first, then finally gave in to her wishes. After tucking the matching gold bands deep into his pants pocket, he took Samantha by the hand and led her out the door.

Time was passing quickly, and Garrett hoped they wouldn't have to wait long to get their license. But to his dismay, the clerk's office in the town hall was mobbed. Visibly agitated, Garrett stood in line with Samantha, wishing they had come here first. When the clerk informed them that there was still a three day waiting period, Samantha was sure Garrett would voice a complaint. But, he didn't. Minutes later they were back on the snowmobile.

* * * * *

To Samantha, it seemed like an eternity before Garrett stopped the vehicle before the cabin of Judge Patrick L. Ryan. His knuckles had barely touched on the heavy wooden barrier, when the door opened slowly and a tiny silver-haired woman came into view.

"Ah, Mr. Garrett and Miss McCall," the woman said, nodding pleasantly. "I'm Mrs. Ryan. Won't you please come in?" She stepped back to let the couple enter. Glancing apprehensively at Garrett, Samantha removed her jacket and hat and placed them in the open arms of the woman.

"Your boots," Mrs. Ryan said, pointing downward. "Wouldn't you be more comfortable without them?"

"Thank you, Mrs. Ryan," Samantha replied, "but I'll just keep them on. They're sort of my good luck charms."

After collecting Garrett's jacket, the judge's wife ushered them into the living room. The spirit of Christmas was everywhere, from the twinkling lights on the tree in the corner of the room, to the Nativity Scene with its porcelain figurines displayed across the entire field-stone mantelpiece. Fixed on the inside of the door was a home-made wreath accentuated by a huge red velvet bow. The cabin itself was much larger than Adam's or Garrett's, and certainly more modernized, giving the distinct impression that this haven in the mountains served as more than just a winter retreat. It was so cozy, so invitingly warm that Samantha voiced her profound admiration to the woman on her decorating skills.

"You're most kind," Mrs. Ryan said, gesturing the couple towards the high winged-back sofa that dominated the spacious, colonial-styled room. "Paddy, that's my husband, and I spend a great deal of time here in the mountains. It's so beautiful in the winter, and just as lovely in the–"

"Is that our bride and groom, Irene?" The low raspy voice came from behind Samantha. Peering over her shoulder, Samantha's eyes widened with incredulity at the short, balding, man who walked with the aid of a cane. The physical resemblance to her father was uncanny, and she couldn't help but feel a momentary pang of sadness as she looked at him.

"I'm truly grateful to you for agreeing to marry us, your honor," Garrett said, extending his hand to the judge, who grasped it firmly.

"Think nothing of it, Mr. Garrett," he replied, looking deeply into Tony's eyes. For some reason, the look seemed to go right through him, and for a split second, Garrett felt somewhat uneasy.

"You kids don't mind if I ask you a very important question, do you?" the elderly man queried, looking at both of them. Garrett and Samantha answered in unison, "Of course not."

The judge leaned heavily on his cane. "The decision to marry is the most important one you will ever make in your life. Are you both certain this is what you really want to do?"

Samantha turned to face her future husband. Dancing shadows from the flames in the hearth caught his handsome face in profile. It brought the pulse to beat rapidly in her throat and stirred her senses. When Garrett met her adoring stare, she said almost breathlessly, "I've never been so sure of anything in my life."

Garrett nodded in agreement. "Nor have I."

"Then let's begin," the judge announced as he moved

past them and stopped before a polished cherry wood desk along the wall by the door. From one of the drawers he extracted a white sheet of paper and a pen. With his back to the couple he asked, "Have you had your blood tests taken?

"Yes, we did," Garrett answered smoothly.

"Fine." Now, I need some information on this license and we can get started."

Garrett spoke up immediately. "I must confess that we just obtained the license, and according to the law, there is a three day waiting period."

"Don't be concerned with that," the judge replied. "I'll be more than happy to waive it." After the slightly nervous couple answered the questions, and thanked the judge for doing them the favor, the older man took his prayer book in hand and gestured the beaming couple to take their places before the hearth. As he readied himself, Mrs. Ryan bustled about the room drawing the short, heavy draperies across the windows. Then, striking a match to a pair of white candles, she placed one at each end of the mantelpiece. The tiny flames bathed the room in a soft golden glow, causing Samantha to barely contain her joy and excitement. In a matter of minutes, she would become Mrs. Tony Garrett. No one in the world was as happy as she.

Time hung suspended as Judge Ryan read from the black leather prayer book, for Samantha was conscious of nothing except the man who stood beside her. In her eyes, he had become larger than life and more handsome, like the mythical god, Adonis. Never, in her life, did she feel so tiny, so fragile, yet so loved as now, when in a slow, smooth voice, Tony said, "I, Anthony Paul Garrett, take you, Samantha Rose McCall, to be my lawful wedded wife..."

When he was through, Samantha repeated the vow in a

calm and steady voice that belied her quavering insides. At the finish, Garrett gave her hand a gentle squeeze, then reached into his pants pocket and produced the gold wedding bands. As soon as the couple slipped the rings on each others finger, the judge pronounced them man and wife.

Warm blue eyes gazed into warmer green, oblivious to everything around them. Garrett wasted no time when he was permitted to kiss his bride. He curved his arms tightly around Samantha's waist and brought his lips down to hers in a long, passionate kiss.

When their lips finally parted, Samantha was breathless.

"Congratulations to both of you," the older couple said in unison. Mrs. Ryan then took the young bride in her arms and hugged her warmly. "I'm so happy for you, my dear," she said, wiping a tear from her eye.

"Now, don't go getting weepy on us, Irene," her husband warned, giving a sly wink to Garrett.

"Oh hush, Paddy," she scolded. "You know weddings always make me cry." Samantha gave a warm smile to the woman, who was now dabbing at her eyes with the hem of her apron.

The congratulations now at an end, Garrett grabbed the judge's hand firmly in his and expressed his appreciation for interrupting his Christmas to perform the ceremony. He was in the process of asking for their jackets, when Mrs. Ryan stepped forward.

"Must you leave immediately?" she asked somewhat disappointed as her gray-blue eyes shifted from Samantha to Garrett. "I've prepared a fine Christmas feast for our children, but the storm has delayed their arrival. Lord knows when they'll get here. In the meantime, it would be a sin to let all this good food go to waste."

"Oh, no, uh ... we couldn't possibly," Samantha said, casting a wary look at her new husband. "We've imposed enough already. Besides, now that the roads are being cleared, your family will be arriving anytime now." It wasn't that Samantha was ungrateful for the invitation, it was that suddenly she wanted to be alone with Tony, back in his cabin, back in his warm embrace.

* * * * *

"Nonsense," the judge protested vehemently. "They have to travel all the way from Montreal. With luck on their side, they won't be here until late tonight or early tomorrow. So, that settles that. You're having Christmas dinner here with us."

Samantha refrained from looking at her husband. If his disappointment was as deep as hers, it might be revealed in his eyes, and she didn't want to see it, for fear she might burst into tears. However, it seemed strange to her that he hadn't persisted when she refused the invitation. Wasn't he as anxious to start their honeymoon as she? Knitting her brows together in perplexity, Samantha shot a baleful look his way. But Garrett deliberately avoided her eyes by turning and walking to the sofa, then easing himself down into the soft cushions. When the judge offered him a glass of eggnog, he accepted graciously. Samantha agreed to one also, fighting off the hopeless feeling that was beginning to gnaw at her insides. They would probably be there the entire afternoon.

Mrs. Ryan summoned her husband to the kitchen, and

Samantha, grateful for the brief respite, took the opportunity to voice her annoyance. "Do you really want to stay, Tony?" she asked, the words trembling on her lips. "I was sure you couldn't wait for us to be alone."

Garrett turned, and Samantha noticed an ominous gleam enter his eyes. His voice bristled. "What's the rush, sweetheart? We've got all night ... forever, for that matter. What's a few hours delay? These people are bending over backwards to make this day memorable for us. The least we can do is show a bit of gratitude."

The look in his eyes made her blood run cold. It was the same look she had encountered that day in the restaurant. It had devastated her then. It was practically destroying her now.

Turning on her heels, she stepped before the hearth and lowered her moist eyes to the crackling flames, ready to indulge in a bit of self-pity. Just then, the judge and his wife returned with their drinks. "I'd like to propose a toast to the bride and groom," the judge announced. "To Samantha and Tony. May their years together be filled with all the good things in life – loyal friends, unfailing good health, and an abundance of love."

"Here, here," Mrs. Ryan returned, and the four brought their glasses to their lips.

Samantha couldn't resist looking at her husband, who was staring back at her. She wondered what thoughts occupied his mind while his smoldering eyes raked her body. Could it be he was regretting his decision to dine with the Ryans? Did he indeed wish they were alone now, cuddled together in their own little love nest? Well, if his thoughts did not run along that course, then she would see to it that they did.

Finishing her drink, Mrs. Ryan left them to enter the dining room. "I believe dinner is about ready," the older man said, and slipping his palm beneath Samantha's elbow, he escorted the bride to the table. Without waiting for her host to assign her seat, Samantha approached the chair beside Garrett's. Turning a warm smile on him, she lowered herself onto the seat.

A feast fit for a king was spread before them, yet Samantha was anything but hungry. The doughnuts and coffee she'd eaten still lay heavily on her stomach, and she groaned at the prospects of having to consume turkey and all the trimmings. The sight and aroma of the bountiful repast brought a lump to her throat, so to divert her attention, she turned to Mrs. Ryan and asked, "How did you manage to cook all this without electricity? Or has the power been restored since this morning?"

Mrs. Ryan took Samantha's dish and began piling food on the delicate blue and white china plate. "We have our own electrical generator," she answered, flashing a generous smile. "It pays to have an electrician for a son, so a power failure doesn't affect us. But I'm sure the problem's been remedied. Repair trucks have been passing by all day." She set the dish before Samantha, then began serving Garrett.

Toying with her food, Samantha waited patiently until her husband brought a fork full of sweet potatoes to his mouth. Just as he was about to swallow, she moved her leg slightly to the left and rubbed it sensuously against his thigh. As she watched the startled expression suddenly appear on his face, she almost burst into laughter. Garrett's complexion went from white to crimson then back to white again.

"Cut it out," he hissed through clenched teeth, trying

hard not to attract the older couple's attention.

But Mrs. Ryan heard him, and with furrowed brows asked, "Did you say something, Mr. Garrett?"

Momentarily flustered, Garrett had to think fast. "Uh ... yes ... uh..." he stammered while lowering his hand beneath the red and white linen table cloth to give Samantha's leg a shove. "I said, without a doubt, yes, that's it. Without a doubt this is the uh ... uh ... finest dinner I've had since I can't remember when." The statement made absolutely no sense, but it both delighted and excited Samantha just to watch him squirm under the scrutinizing gaze of the judge and his wife.

However, Garrett was too much the professional to remain in a ridiculous situation for long. Clearing his throat, he explained with a grin, "What I meant was that I haven't enjoyed a satisfying home cooked meal since I left New York City nearly two weeks ago." His grin widened as his gaze swept over Samantha.

"Touché," she murmured, her lips curving into a smirk.

Satisfied with the brief explanation, Mrs. Ryan resumed serving her husband. When the judge carved a hearty serving of turkey and set it on Garrett's plate, Samantha pushed the dish closer to him. "Then you'd better take advantage of Mrs. Ryan's culinary talents, my love," she teased devilishly, "because cooking is not one of my strong points."

Patrick Ryan roared from behind his napkin. "I don't think Tony is much likely to care. Not for the first six months."

The older woman cast an ominous glance at her husband, who continued to laugh heartily. "Pay him no

138

mind, my dear," she said to Samantha who glowed with color. "It's the brandy in the eggnog that's doing the talking. Paddy's usually not so forward with strangers."

The judge put his napkin aside. "Tony is hardly a stranger to me, Irene. Think back to the fourth of July about two years ago. I performed the wedding ceremony between Tony's best friend, Charlie Austin and his ex-wife, Rosemary. Don't you remember? You witnessed that wedding just as you did this one."

Mrs. Ryan was quick to respond to her husband, but Samantha heard none of the conversation between the two. She had withdrawn into the shadowy corner of her mind where the faceless image of Charlie Austin hovered within. Admittedly, she didn't know the man the judge spoke of and yet, somehow his name seemed all too familiar. Reaching a blank conclusion, Samantha blurted out, "That name rings a bell, but I can't seem to place him."

Judge Ryan was quick to enlighten her. He's a writer. Mysteries, I believe. For a while his books were on the bestseller's list. Anyway, Charlie told me that he and Tony had become rivals over Rosemary. She left Tony for Charlie. Since both men were well known, the news spread like wildfire." He cast a disdainful look at Garrett whose face had suddenly turned to stone.

Samantha noticed a sneer form on the judge's lips as he continued his taunt. "Rumor has it you've never forgiven him for stealing Rosemary away from you."

All eyes turned to Garrett, who was trying diligently to keep his growing anger in check. It was painfully obvious to Samantha that he was close to the breaking point. The tendons strained beneath his wide jaw, and a muscle twitched spasmodically in his cheek.

When he finally spoke, his words were like thunder. "God dammit, Ryan, I see right through you! But you're wasting your time! I remember you, too. Now, if you have a bone to pick with me, then be man enough to come out with it. But don't sit there and embarrass my wife on our wedding day with your tasteless gossip!"

Then, with lips grim in vexation, he turned to his bride. "I believe we've overstayed our welcome."

A look of horror crossed Samantha's face. What was going on here? Why were these two men, who seemed so amicable just minutes ago, suddenly at each other's throats? If Tony was upset because the judge hit a raw nerve when he mentioned his ex-wife, then she could almost understand his hostile attitude. This was hardly the time or place to hit on that touchy subject. But, why should it stir such anger in the judge?

Feeling terribly confused, yet wanting to make peace between the two men, if only for the sake of Mrs. Ryan, who looked as if she were ready to faint, she turned to her embittered husband. "But- but Tony, we can't leave now, not in the middle of dinner." Astounded by their blatant behavior, she fixed wide eyes on Garrett, then on the older man. "I'm sure the judge wouldn't have mentioned your friend, had he known it would upset you so."

But the judge ignored her intervention, and when he jumped to his feet, Samantha gasped aloud.

"My apologies to you, my dear, for upsetting your wedding day," he said, his piercing dark eyes fixed not on her but on Garrett. "But I've waited a long time for this moment, Garrett, and now that it's come, I'm giving you a flat out warning. Keep your investigators away from the District Attorney's office!"

140

"District Attorney's office?" Samantha echoed incredulously. "What are you talking about?" She turned horrified eyes on Garrett. "Tony, what is he talking about? What does that have to do with your friend?"

"It has nothing to do with Charlie," Garrett replied, shrugging her off. Then, rising to his full height, he slid back his chair and walked slowly around the table, stopping inches from the infuriated old man. Fire blazed in Garrett's eyes, and he could feel the color in his face change from tan to ashen gray. To punctuate his vexation, he grasped the judge's napkin, then flung it back down on the table.

"I should have remembered the name when the manager of the coffee shop gave it to me, but at the time I was just not thinking. Then, when I heard your smooth voice on the phone and I remembered who you were, I should have guessed this was the moment you were waiting for," he growled. "How foolish of me not to have anticipated your ulterior motive in getting me here. Foolish man. You have succeeded in accomplishing nothing by flinging this unwarranted ultimatum at me, because I'm not responsible for bringing to light the machinations within the District Attorney's office. That honor belongs to the *Daily News*. Now, if you're not involved – and this is off the record, but I believe that you are – then come on my show. You will be given ample opportunity to dispel the rumors of political corruption that has surfaced in the last month. I believe the *Daily News* is on to something. So now the ball is in your court. What are you going to do about it?"

Without waiting for an answer, he turned to Mrs. Ryan, who was close to tears. "If you will kindly get our jackets," he said, avoiding the elderly woman's eyes.

At the door, Samantha was embraced warmly by Mrs.

141

Ryan, who apologized profusely for the disastrous conclusion to what had started out as a wonderful day. Her eyes brimming with tears, Samantha looked beyond the woman to Patrick Ryan, who had taken a seat by the fire. For a moment the old man and the young girl stared at each other, neither of them uttering a word, yet the sardonic gleam in his eyes spoke volumes. He was not the least bit remorseful for having shattered her wedding day. In fact, he was pleased with himself ... utterly and delightfully pleased.

Too upset now to even thank the woman for her hospitality, Samantha rushed past her husband, pulled open the door, and ran from the cabin.

CHAPTER TEN

After giving the cabin door an impatient slam, Garrett marched straight to the hearth and built a fire. Visibly irritated, he poked at the burning wood, then removed his jacket and flung it on the chair beside him. "I need a drink," he declared hotly as he stalked towards the kitchen.

"I'd say you need a couple," Samantha retorted, tossing her jacket over the side of the bed.

The acid tone of her voice caused Garrett to stop dead in his tracks. His face fixed in a tight scowl, he turned to her. "What's that supposed to mean?"

By this time, Samantha had had enough. Her nerves were coiled up tight and ready to snap. Fast on the verge of tears, she challenged ungraciously, "You tell me! You're the one who needs the drink!" She shivered uncontrollably in her anger. "I know it has nothing to do with the altercation over the D.A.'s office. You had the judge in your back pocket and you know it. *I* believe you're still furious with Charlie for stealing your wife."

Garrett's mood was again mocking and cruel. "I've had enough head-to-head combat for one day, young lady," he sneered. "I'd appreciate it if you'd just drop it!"

Samantha squared her shoulders. "I will not drop it! From the looks of you, I'd say the judge and I both hit the nail on the head. You've *never* forgiven your friend for what he did to you. And, I'll go one step further. You can deny it all you want, but you don't fool me. You're still in love with her. That's why you need the drink – to forget. So, why the hell did you marry *me*?"

143

A tic beat furiously in Garrett's cheek, and he lowered his lids over mocking eyes. "Your sarcasm is not warranted. Neither is a response to your ridiculous accusation."

Samantha ignored the brush-off. "A refusal to answer a statement usually implies guilt. So why don't you just admit it and get it over with?"

With one swift move he came to her and clasped both hands on her upper arms. His look was rough and unyielding, and Samantha thought he might hurt her. She tried unsuccessfully to break free. But she was no match for a man of his size. When he pulled her closer, she fell against him, weak and trembling. His burning lips brushed lightly against hers, making her head reel as he clutched her tightly to him. Moaning softly, he lifted her up into his arms and placed her on the sofa cushions.

"I'll say this once and only once. Rosemary means nothing to me. She's a part of my past that's over and done with. I married you because I love you."

"So why did you practically attack the judge for mentioning her name?

Garrett gave an exasperated sigh. "Ryan was simply displaying his cunningness. He knows I know he's guilty. He's scared. Damn scared. And he's got good reason to be. My mistake was in tipping my hand and revealing my next course of action. I could kick myself for doing that. Nevertheless, I'm a thorn in his side, and he thought by giving me an ultimatum, I'd back off. Now as far as you and I are concerned, Ryan tried to destroy our marriage before it even began. Looks to me like he almost succeeded."

His emotions were now too strong to be ignored. "Forgive me for taking my anger out on you, tonight of all nights," he apologized softly. "I hope you won't let all that's happened spoil–"

"Do you think there's a chance he could be innocent?"

Garrett gave it some thought. "Not according to the evidence I have." He drew her closer to him and began nibbling on her bottom lip. "Let's forget about him, honey," he whispered. "I've got better things on my mind. Now tell me, don't you have something more alluring to wear than this suit?"

"As a matter of fact, I have," she teased, pressing her mouth to his cheek. Immediately, Garrett claimed possession of her moist, parted lips, and for Samantha, it was sweet torture. Unwillingly, she drew back from him. "It'll just take a few minutes. Don't go away now, ya hear?" she taunted gaily, then slid from his embrace and scurried to the bedroom.

As soon as she closed the door, Samantha expelled a hearty gasp. The bedroom was freezing, and the only window that should have permitted light for her to change by, was thick with frost. Suddenly, she remembered Mrs. Ryan stating that the electrical power was sure to have been restored. The instant her fingers touched the switch on the wall beside the door, the room was thrown into a blaze of light. Giving a sigh of relief, she opened her suitcase on the bed and searched through the folded garments. There it was – her lacy pink peignoir. It felt soft as a cloud, and she smiled wickedly imagining the look of pleasure that was sure to appear on Tony's face once she waltzed back into the room. Laying the nightgown on top of the bed, she began to undress. She was just about to remove her slacks when she took notice of her open-toed shoes. In her haste to escape from the Ryan's cabin, she had forgotten Adam's boots. "Oh, well," she sighed, kicking off the slacks. She'd get

Adam a new pair later on.

Clad now in the long, flowing peignoir, Samantha reached into the top pocket of her suitcase and withdrew a pair of pink satin ribbons. Previously fashioned to wear with a sweater of the identical color, the ribbons were now the appropriate touch Samantha wanted as she combed her hair up into two long, thick ponytails. Securing the ribbons in place, she gave an affirmative nod to her reflection in the mirror above the bureau. She wanted to look like the provocative woman-child Garrett had been taken with that night in the studio. She then placed a touch of cologne behind each ear. She was ready.

A shiver of sensual delight danced over her as she padded barefoot across the room towards the door. Just as her hand clasped around the doorknob, Samantha became aware of voices in the other room. Imagining her husband had decided to turn on the radio, she gave it little thought, until the voices became more pronounced.

One was definitely Garrett's. There was no question that the other belonged to a woman. Pressing her ear firmly against the door, Samantha's breath caught in her throat as she heard him speak in a low, controlled tone. "How did you find me?"

"It wasn't easy, darling."

Darling? The word hit upon Samantha's brain like a hammer. Who would be calling her husband darling? For a fleeting moment she was tempted to dash into the living room and confront the impertinent intruder. But when the conversation resumed, Samantha could do nothing but stand there, paralyzed.

"Answer my question!" he commanded coldly. "Who told you I was here?"

"Now is that anyway to greet me, darling? And on Christmas Day?" the woman asked in a drawl. "I've gone to a lot of trouble to get here. The least you could do is offer me a drink and a chance to warm up by the fire."

Garrett's voice bristled. "You shouldn't be cold, Rosemary. Not in a ten-thousand-dollar mink coat."

Rosemary! Samantha gasped at hearing the woman's name. Why would Rosemary be tracking Tony down? Squelching down a wave of nausea that suddenly gripped her, Samantha inched open the door, her curiosity now more intense than her queasiness. She just had to get a look at that woman!

Taking care not to make a sound, she opened the door wider and looked around, but her view was obscured by the monstrous Christmas tree. *Drat!* She balled her fists in frustration. She was almost resigned to her place in the doorway, when she remembered seeing a small foot stool beneath the sink in the bathroom. If she could make her way quietly along the wall, she could get the stool, secure it behind the tree, and observe them without their knowledge.

She admitted that in stooping to the level of a voyeur, she might be detected in her risky endeavor, but that was the chance she would have to take. Now was not the time to be timid.

Seconds later, her mission successfully accomplished, Samantha balanced herself on the stool, congratulating herself on her ingenuity. Her view was totally unobscured now. She glared at her husband and Rosemary, who stood with her back to Samantha. Though her face was hidden, it was obvious the woman was beautiful, because Garrett's eyes were glued to her as though he were caught in her spell. It didn't matter that a moment ago he was curt and

147

annoyed by her unexpected arrival. Right now, he was captivated by her. So much so that it took all of Samantha's willpower not to send the tree crashing down upon his head. It would serve him right, she thought furiously.

Rosemary's voice commanded Samantha's attention. "Why are you being so difficult, darling? We've been over this a hundred times."

"Precisely," Garrett replied, shaking his head as if to ward off the spell. "But as usual, you disregard what you don't want to hear. So, you've wasted your time and energy by making this trip. Now, turn around and get out!"

Rosemary shrugged off Garrett's dismissal by putting her arms around his neck. "Kiss me, you sexy tiger," she taunted, raising her lips to his. "We both know I'm not going anywhere."

Garrett responded by pushing her arms away. "I'm married, Rosemary." he stated bluntly.

A low, throaty laugh came from the woman. "That's nonsense, darling, but I forgive your little white lie. You always did love to play hard to get. Not that your ridiculous fabrication discourages me. In fact, it turns me on. Just as *you* turn me on."

Her arms circled Garrett's neck again, and she pressed her lips passionately to his.

A gasp of horror nearly escaped Samantha, who had to clasp her hand over her mouth to silence it. The nerve of that woman, kissing *her* husband! But when Garrett's arms went around Rosemary's waist, and he pulled her closer, Samantha felt ashamed and degraded beyond description.

How dare he declare his love for her one minute, then savor his ex-wife's kisses the next! It was enough to make Samantha want to carve out his heart with her fingernails and present it to the overly-aggressive hussy.

Indignant to the bone, Samantha was ready to step down and call a halt to this passionate love scene, when she saw Garrett push Rosemary away with such force that the startled woman nearly backed into the Christmas tree.

"I didn't lie about my being married," he declared derisively, "I am. And you got your kiss, now leave. You see, Rosemary, you don't turn *me* on."

With deliberate slowness, Rosemary moved toward him, removed her coat and tossed it on the chair. As she did, Samantha caught a full view of the blonde, statuesque woman. Garbed in a black, low-cut sweater and slacks, she was every bit the sophisticated beauty Samantha expected. Round, full breasts strained beneath her sweater, while her curvaceous hips swayed sensuously, drawing Samantha's eyes downward to her long, shapely legs as she perched herself on the edge of the sofa bed.

"C'mon, darling," Rosemary beckoned seductively, extending both arms to him. "You know you want me the way you always did, otherwise you wouldn't have kissed me. Besides..."

She turned her head and looked around the room. "I see no signs of a wife anywhere. So give up this ridiculous fight and let's make use of this sorry excuse for a bed."

With lightening speed, Rosemary cast off her sweater and slacks and slid onto the soft, sofa cushions, out of Samantha's range of sight. Frustrated at not being able to keep an eye on the two of them at the same time, Samantha parted the branches slightly. When that failed to broaden her scope, she stood up on tip toe, stretching far beyond her capacity to remain steady. Her weight now unevenly distributed, the stool tipped over on its side and gave away from beneath her.

Realizing the disaster that was about to happen, she panicked and automatically grabbed at the branches to keep from falling. But her frantic movements pushed the tree forward, sending it crashing down along the foot of the sofa bed.

In all her glory, Samantha lay sprawled across the piercing pine needles, tinsel, and garlands. An anguished cry escaped her lips, not from the pain of the fall, but from the embarrassment of being discovered. Mortified, she once again wished the ground would open up and swallow her.

Garrett, too stunned to move, stared with incredulity at his scantily-clad bride as she lifted herself up and began to free herself from the tangled mess. But when a roar of laughter erupted from Rosemary, Samantha stopped short. Blind fury burned in her eyes as she glared at the woman tucked beneath the quilt, holding her sides against the hysterics that did not subside until the thunderous roar of Garrett's voice sliced the air. "Put your clothes on and get out!"

Rosemary dragged her eyes to Garrett. "Who are you talking to, darling," she mocked, "Mary Poppins here, or me?" Before giving him a chance to respond, Rosemary's gaze switched from Garrett back to Samantha. "Well, he's not looking at *me*, Miss – er–"

"It's *Mrs.* Garrett!" Samantha snapped, taking an angry step forward, only to be halted by the tree. Rosemary's gaze switched back to Garrett, and she laughed again. "Don't tell me you've taken to robbing the cradle just to make me jealous, darling."

"For God's sake, Rosemary, shut up!" Garrett bellowed, his face now the color of chalk.

Samantha placed her hands on her hips. "Oh, let Rosemary have her say, *darling,*" she said coldly, trying to keep her anger in check. "This is getting better by the minute."

Totally flustered, Garrett ran agitated fingers through his hair. "Listen to me, honey," he pleaded. "This is not what you think. Rosemary and I are *not* lovers!"

"Oh, yes we are!" Rosemary contradicted, casting an ominous gleam to Samantha. "Why else would I be here?"

Out of control now, Garrett lunged toward his bride, pushing aside the tree in his haste to reach her.

"Don't come any closer, Tony!" Samantha warned, snatching up the stool and holding it before her.

"Don't listen to Rosemary, honey!" he ordered. "She's crazy! Can't you see that?"

"*I'm* the one who's crazy!" Samantha spit back, her voice cracking on a note of hysteria. "Crazy for believing in you and your lies!"

"I've never lied to you. I swear it!" He was practically begging her to believe him. "None of this–"

"Has Tony been in love with you all along?" Samantha asked the woman, cutting Garrett's explanation off short.

"Since the day we first met." Rosemary snickered victoriously.

"Then he's all yours," Samantha hissed in return.

Turning back to Garrett, her tone bitter and accusing she stated, "I'll see you in court, *darling!*" With that, she turned on her heels, dashed back into the bedroom, and locked the door behind her. There was no time to give in to the flood of emotions she was feeling. She just wanted to leave before he was able to stop her.

Flinging off her peignoir, she dressed hurriedly. When

she was through, she yanked open the window, tossed her suitcase out into the snow, and climbed out after it.

Forgetting about the new brown boots that were tucked into one of the pockets in the suitcase, she had slipped into her open-toed high heels. The minute her feet sank into the deep snow, she gave a tormented cry. With only a sweater to shield her from the freezing temperature, she began to shiver uncontrollably.

"Need some help, little lady?"

"Oh, yes, please," she cried, looking away from the bright lights that blinded her. She couldn't see the face of the man who had suddenly appeared like an angel from heaven.

"Where are you—"

"Quick," she interrupted him, practically breathless. "Take me away before he..."

The man didn't need to hear any more. He picked her up as though she were weightless and tossed her into the front of the truck. Then tossing her suitcase onto her lap, he was behind the wheel before she had a chance to catch her breath.

"Are you all right?" he asked, putting the snowplow into gear.

"Yes," she whispered gratefully, nodding. When she realized she had left her purse with her jacket in the living room, she stammered, "I-I don't have my pocketbook with me, so I can't pay you, but could you take me down the road about a quarter of a mile?"

"How about we stop at the clinic first?" he asked, watching her shiver. "You might be frostbitten."

"That won't be necessary," she said, looking at the burly young man. "I'm okay, thanks to you."

As the man turned the plow and passed the front of the cabin, Samantha saw Garrett standing in the open doorway. "Is that the man you're running from?

The word came out on a sob. "Yes."

* * * * *

"Good Lord, child!" Mrs. Ryan exclaimed the moment her eyes set upon the half-frozen girl. "Come inside, quickly." She set the luggage down by the door and whisked Samantha into the living room and over to the fireplace where Judge Ryan sat dozing in his easy chair. His eyes flew open when her wet slacks touched the side of his leg. Sitting upright, he encountered her trembling form.

"What's wrong, Samantha? Why have you come back?" He gave a quick look around the room expecting to find Garrett. When he saw she was alone, he looked at her oddly. "Where's your husband?"

"Y-you mean my soon-to-be-ex-husband," she stammered, twisting her hands over the flames.

Patrick Ryan turned to his wife. "Irene, get her a brandy, fast!"

Mrs. Ryan scurried into the kitchen, then returned immediately with the drink. After giving the older woman a nod of gratitude, Samantha took the glass and slumped into a stuffed chair opposite the judge. As soon as she took a swallow of the tart beverage, her body went limp, and she shuddered at the burning sensation that filled her chest. It wasn't until the glass was empty that she finally stopped trembling.

"I've left Tony," she said, choking back a sob.

"Why?" the old man asked.

153

The image of Rosemary kissing her husband was the first agonizing picture that shot into her mind. "B-because," she said with difficulty, "Tony is with Rosemary right now. I believe he was expecting her. He swears he wasn't. I asked her point blank if they'd been lovers all along. She said yes. Tony denies it. I-I just had to leave. I didn't know where else to go. I'm sorry to have involved both of you in this, but–"

"How did you get here?" Mrs. Ryan asked, wringing her hands in her apron.

Samantha looked up at her. "A man in a snowplow."

Patrick Ryan had heard enough. "That dirty, no good, son-of-a–"

"Now, now, Paddy," Irene Ryan interrupted. "Remember your blood pressure. Getting upset isn't going to help Samantha."

"Never mind my blood pressure!" he balked gruffly. "I've got a good mind to go right over there and–"

"No!" Samantha clasped a hand over her mouth. "Please don't do that! Please! The two of you are at odds to begin with. I don't want anymore trouble."

Judge Ryan considered it for a moment, then leaned back into his seat. Looking at her, he could see the torment in her eyes. Damping his anger down he said, "You realize Garrett's going to come here for you. The question is, what do you plan to do?"

Just as she was about to answer, there came a furious pounding on the door. It brought Samantha and the judge bolting to their feet. "He's here!" she exclaimed, her heart racing. "I don't want to see him. Please. Don't let him take me back there."

Mrs. Ryan embraced the young girl warmly. "Come

with me, my dear. I'll take you into the bedroom." Leading Samantha away, the elderly woman turned to her husband. "You'd better let him in before he breaks down the door."

Safely hidden away, Samantha leaned weakly against the bedroom door. Within seconds, she heard Tony and the judge engaging in a verbal duel.

"Where's my wife, Ryan?" Garrett roared. "I know she's here."

"She doesn't want to see you," the judge replied, his voice more controlled than Garrett's.

"She doesn't know what she wants right now, and that's understandable," Garrett returned. "She's had quite a surprise thrown at her. For that matter, so have I."

"Really!" the judge drawled. "And what will you do if I refuse to turn her over to you? Tear my house apart until you find her?"

"Don't push me, Ryan," Garrett warned. "This is none of your business, so stay out of it!"

"Samantha came here for refuge," the older man pointed out. "That makes it my business. Now get the hell out! If your wife wants you, she knows where to find you."

Garrett flashed back angrily, "I'm not leaving here without her, and I'll wait if it takes all night!"

"You'll leave, and *now*!" the judge insisted. "If I have to call the police to remove you bodily, I will. You're in *my* house now and I'll have you arrested for trespassing. Do I make myself clear?"

The slamming of the door issued Garrett's angry departure. Sighing forlornly, Samantha re-entered the living room. As she approached the judge, she lowered her gaze to the floor. "I'm so sorry you had to be brought into this," she apologized weakly. "I realize it put you on the spot."

She felt so terrible about the whole thing she would have gone on apologizing forever if the judge hadn't stopped her. "Don't be concerned about it," he said, a triumphant gleam appearing once again in his dark eyes. "For me, it was a pleasure...a real pleasure."

* * * * *

Four hours had passed since Garrett and the judge had locked horns for the second time. Four hours that seemed like four years.

During that time Samantha had instructed the judge to try to contact her agent, Adam Pearce. He had succeeded, and now she sat, curled up on the sofa, waiting for him to arrive.

When Adam finally got there, it was well past midnight. "I-I came as quickly as possible," he stammered nervously, taking in Samantha's solemn face from his spot in the doorway. "The roads are treacherous. It was a crawl all the way."

"Then perhaps you should stay the night," Mrs. Ryan suggested, her eyes darting from Samantha to Adam.

"Thank you kindly, Mrs. Ryan," Samantha said, pulling on the jacket Garrett had brought with him for her return to his lodge. "But, I've imposed upon your hospitality enough for one day." She turned from the woman and gave a final glance around the room. How warm and festive it had been that afternoon when she and Garrett had exchanged wedding vows. Now, in the middle of the night, it seemed as cold and empty as she. Samantha suppressed a sob. None of it seemed real.

The old man took her in his arms and embraced her

warmly. "I'm sorry it turned out so badly for you, my dear," he said, and a part of her wanted desperately to believe he was being sincere. But when she looked into his dark eyes, she saw the triumphant look of victory. "Remember, everything happens for the best," he continued. "You're too fine a lady for the likes of him."

Feeling wretched and miserable inside, Samantha bade a last farewell to the couple. Then, rushing past them, she dashed out into the night and climbed into the tiny red Volkswagen.

Adam Pearce was right behind her. After placing her luggage on the back seat, he dropped the black boots onto her feet. "Here," he said. "The lady said you forgot these. Put them on. The heater still doesn't work. And by the way, we've got to go back up the road past both our cabins. It's the only way to the highway."

His words fell on deaf ears. She was busy wondering if Rosemary's car was still parked outside Garrett's lodge. But as the Volkswagen rolled along the roadway and neared his cabin, she discovered, to her relief, no car in sight. There was only a faint ray of light coming from one of the cabin's tiny windows. Ironically, it seemed to beckon her. With all her heart she wanted to run to her husband ... to his strong arms, never to leave him again. Adam, seeming to sense her desire, slowed the car down to a crawl, but her pride won out. "Speed it up, Adam," she choked, looking straight ahead. "We're a long way from home."

CHAPTER ELEVEN

Not a word passed between them for the better part of an hour. Adam couldn't tolerate the silence any longer. "Tell me what happened, Red, and don't shrug me off."

Samantha arched a fine brow at him. "Didn't the judge fill you in?"

He tightened his grip on the wheel. "All Ryan said was that he'd married the two of you in the afternoon, but tonight Garrett's ex-wife showed up on his doorstep, and now you want to go back to New York." He pursed his lips together and shrugged his shoulders. "I can understand that you're upset, but why the hell are you running away? She can't mean anything to him if he married you."

"You'd think that, wouldn't you?" she responded angrily. "But you'd be wrong. I saw him kiss her, Adam, the way a man in love kisses a woman."

Adam's eyes opened wide. "I know I'm gonna regret asking this, but where were you when this action was taking place?"

"I was standing on a stool, hiding behind the Christmas tree."

Adam shook his head in disbelief and sighed heavily. "Give me strength." Samantha started to explain when he cut her off. "Are you telling me that when this woman arrived, you took off and hid behind the tree? Why? You had nothing to hide. You're married to the guy!"

"I didn't run and hide when Rosemary came to the door!" she fumed, outraged. "I was in the bedroom changing my clothes. I heard voices – a man's and a

158

woman's – coming from the living room. They were arguing at first. And then I heard her call him *darling*. So, I snuck out of the room and hid behind the tree. But I couldn't see anything, so I got the footstool from the bathroom and–"

"Say no more," he groaned. "I can guess the rest."

Tears of humiliation sprung to the surface. "Twice," she whispered, shaking her head disbelievingly, while dabbing at her eyes.

"Huh?"

She leaned over and put her mouth close to his ear. "I said, *twice!* I knocked the damn tree over twice! Can you hear me now?"

"Everybody in these mountains can hear you," he mocked, and there was no mistaking his determination now. "For God's sake, drop the hostility bit and tell me why you two didn't patch things up!"

Immediately, her mood swing went from belligerent to totally distraught. "There I was in all my glory, buried beneath a blue spruce, looking like a prize fool and feeling even worse, while this snow bunny throws off her clothes and hops into Tony's bed, all ready and waiting to make love to *my* husband! What else could I do but leave?"

Adam's brows creased in perplexity. "And Garrett just let you go? He didn't try to stop you?"

"Sure he did," she said. "He tried to explain that the woman was crazy and that I shouldn't jump to conclusions. But–"

"I didn't mean that. I meant, physically try to stop you. He knew your only way out was the bedroom window, so, all he had to do was walk out the front door and go around to the back. And, I don't care how fast you moved. By the time you got undressed, then redressed, opened the window, threw your suitcase out, then climbed out after it, Garrett had enough time to leave the cabin, change the oil in his car, and be at the window before you hit the snow." He shook his head in wonderment. "I still can't understand why he didn't go after you. Not after all the trouble he went through to get you there. It just doesn't make sense."

Suddenly, the car began to skid on the icy pavement, diverting Adam's attention for a minute. When he finally got the car under control, he went on. "After everything that happened at Ryans', why did you go there? Why didn't you go back to my cabin?

Samantha couldn't look at him. "In the first place, I left my purse at Tony's, so I didn't have the key to your cabin. And by the way, the reason I left your place was because the water pipes burst. The lodge is flooded."

"Swell," he groaned. "Now I gotta get a plumber up there." He glanced at her and apologized, "Sorry. Go on with this soap opera."

"My only choice *was* the Ryans."

He leaned towards her for a moment. "How did you get there?"

"When I climbed out the window, I fell in the snow, and like a miracle, a snowplow was going by. The driver took me there."

"Sounds like a bona fide miracle to me," he said under his breath.

Just then, an overpowering chill began to soar through Samantha, so she pulled her jacket tighter around herself and crouched down in the corner by the door. "No more questions, Adam," she said impatiently. "I'm exhausted, and I don't feel well. I must be coming down with a cold."

Adam didn't press the issue. He stopped the car by the

160

side of the road, reached behind to the back seat, grabbed a woolen blanket, and tucked it around her. The next time Samantha opened her eyes, it was nearly dawn. Her head pounding, she took in her surroundings. "Where are we?"

"We're at my place," he said, flexing his tired muscles.

Samantha tried to sit up, but her head seemed weighted with lead. It dropped back heavily against the back of the seat. "I can't stay here," she declared weakly. "Take me back to the hotel."

He pressed an ungloved hand to her brow. "You've got a fever. Best you stay here where I can keep an eye on you."

Samantha felt too sick to argue. When Adam extracted her luggage from the back seat, he then guided her out of the car and into the dimly lit foyer of the exclusive apartment building. She barely remembered the elevator ride or the room she was eventually led to. Neither did she put up a struggle when Adam removed her outer clothing, slipped her into one of his pajama tops, and tucked her into bed.

It was late afternoon before Samantha regained consciousness. Feeling far from refreshed, she lay there like a lump, her throat burning and her nose stuffy and streaming. She closed her eyes again, only to open them wide when she heard Adam at the bedroom door.

"Wake up, sleeping beauty!" Adam chimed enthusiastically as he came to her side and attempted to force a thermometer into her mouth. With one swift hand, she pushed it aside. "I'm okay!" she snapped ungraciously. "I'm well enough to get dressed and get out of here."

"You're not going anywhere!" The lightness in his tone was gone. Ignoring his protest, she tried to swing back the covers, but being devoid of strength, her hand dropped listlessly back onto the bed.

Adam placed a wad of tissues in her palm. "There's a glass of orange juice and a bowl of soup on the night table," he informed her. "Can you manage it alone, or do I have to spoon feed you like a nanny?"

A series of sneezes erupted simultaneously, adding more pressure to her already pounding head. When she used up the tissues, she shoved them back into his hand. "That's for you, Florence Nightingale," she wheezed. "Now be a good sport and hand me that telephone. I want to make a reservation on the next flight out to Tampa."

Adam pulled a face. "Nothing doing, young lady. Like it or not, you're stuck here in New York for the next two days."

She cast watery eyes at him. "No, I'm not. I'm going home, Adam, and that's final!"

He clicked his tongue impatiently. "If it were up to me, I'd put you on a plane tonight, cold or no cold. But your impaired health has nothing to do with it. You're being kept here on business."

Intrigued by that bit of information, Samantha managed to lift herself up on one elbow. "What kind of business? If you mean the manuscript, it's done."

Adam eased himself down onto the side of the bed. "Since you've been gone, the station's been swamped with calls from viewers who are demanding your return on Garrett's show. His producer's been frantic, waiting for this storm to be over. He knew you and Garrett were up in the mountains. If things didn't work out between you two, Garrett was supposed to call me on Christmas Eve. Naturally, he couldn't. But when I didn't hear from him the next day, I felt confident enough to assume you two had hit it off nicely. So, I set it up with Polcheck for you to guest on the show the day after tomorrow."

Samantha was incensed. "How could you do such a thing without consulting me first?"

Adam's cheeks turned red. "I tried to call Garrett at the lodge, but the lines were down. I just told you that," he explained. "When I finally got through yesterday afternoon, there was no answer. Seeing that it was Christmas, I saw no harm in waiting one more day, which is today. I was going–"

"You didn't answer my question," she interrupted.

Exasperated, Adam drew a deep sigh. "I assumed by now you had abandoned that ridiculous fantasy about wanting to get even with him. That was part of the plan – to get the two of you together to iron out your differences. Once that was accomplished, I was positive you'd give your okay, and the interview would sail along beautifully. Garrett would treat you with kid gloves, the viewers would get what they wanted, and I would be able to sit back and relax for the first time since I met you." His lips tightened in a grim line. "You've been quite a handful, you know."

Samantha clutched the pillow beside her. "Well, you assumed wrong. Now call the studio and cancel me out. I'm going home to make arrangements to get an annulment from the gigolo I married."

A wave of dizziness took hold of her, and she eased herself back onto the pillows. She wished Adam would just go away. "Let me rest," she pleaded. "Not only do I have to shake this cold, I have to figure out how I'm going to tell my family about the mess I've made of my life."

Adam quietly left the room.

163

Alone with her thoughts, she wondered how she was going to break the news of her elopement to her family, and then top it off by admitting it was a mistake and now she wanted it annulled. She knew explaining Rosemary's part in all of this would be a monumental task. How do you tell your folks that your new husband is still involve with his ex-wife?

The more she thought about it, the more her head ached. Snuggling deeper under the covers, she decided to worry about it tomorrow ... on the plane ... after a good night's sleep. Surprisingly, she slept like a log, but when the alarm she had set for 5:00 a.m. shrilled in the darkness, she awoke feeling as sick as ever. Moaning, she was about to get out of bed when Adam gave a gentle knock at the door. Without waiting to be invited in, he entered the room.

"More bad news," he said, coming to the foot of the bed.

"What now?" she grated.

Adam thrust his hands into the pockets of his robe. "If you look out the window, you'll see we're having an ice storm. It started about an hour ago. You'd better check with the airport to see if the planes have been grounded."

Samantha's green eyes flashed with anger. "This can't be happening to me! It just can't! She flung herself across the bed and grabbed the telephone. When she got through to the airport, she learned that all flights out of New York City were being canceled. The best they could do was to put her on stand-by. When she hung up the receiver, she gave Adam an ominous look.

"I'd say the gods are against my leaving this place."

Adam curtly replied, "Perhaps for once they're on my side."

She gave a harsh sigh. "This changes nothing. I'm not going on that show!"

Adam gave her a sour look. "There's coffee on the stove. Care to join me if you can get up?" He left without waiting for an answer.

She got up on wobbly legs, grabbed an old robe of Adam's that hung on the back of the door, and joined him in the kitchen. He had already poured the coffee into stone mugs and was filling a small pitcher with milk when Samantha took a seat at the table. Refusing his offer to take more nourishment, she sipped the hot coffee almost greedily.

"You still look awful," he quipped, taking a seat beside her. The Tiffany light above the table was dimmed, but not so much as to hide the haggard look on his face. If she allowed herself to look at him for any length of time, she was afraid she might soften to the point where she would probably agree to at least think about staying in New York. So, she forced her gaze to her coffee mug.

"Going home is the right thing to do," she said forcibly.

"If you say so."

"I do have my pride."

"Right."

"No wife would hang around after being humiliated the way I was."

"You deserve better."

"Absolutely."

"He should hang in Central Park by his toes and let the dogs use him as a relieving post."

"It would serve him right," she agreed heartily.

"I never liked the guy."

"I love him." The unconscious remark made her mouth drop open.

"Aha!" Adam exclaimed, a fire lighting his eyes as he pointed his spoon at her. "I knew I'd get you to admit it!"

"You're incorrigible!" she fired.

"And you're a stubborn, red-headed idiot!"

"He made a fool of me!" she countered defiantly. "He used me to get even with that ... that ... bleached-blonde floozy!"

A deep frown creased Adam's brow. "Where did you get a crazy idea like that?"

"His ex said so," she remarked seriously. "She accused Tony of robbing the cradle just to make her jealous. Well, now she can have him back, lock, stock, and barrel."

"So, you're letting her win without putting up a fight?" Adam persisted.

Samantha rose unsteadily to her feet. "What's to fight? He's in love with her, whether he wants to admit it or not. I'll never, *never* forget the way he grabbed her and kissed her!"

"You're over-reacting girl, and what's worse is you never gave him a chance to have his say."

"Think what you want," she stated firmly. "The marriage that never was, is over!" With that outburst, she ended the conversation by stalking back to the bedroom.

Collapsing on the bed, she buried her face into the pillows and allowed her pent-up tears to flow freely. It was the first time she had abandoned herself wholly to her anguish and despair. But, even as her body shook with heavy, muffled sobs, she refused to renege on her decision. She was going home.

Sheer exhaustion overtook her, and she fell into a

troubled, restless sleep.

* * * * *

The piercing cackle of Rosemary's laughter brought Samantha to the brink of wakefulness. Over and over, the woman taunted mercilessly, "Tony loves me. Me! *Me!*"

"*No ... please!*" Samantha begged her husband, whose eyes were fixed on the woman who moved sensuously in his bed. He ignored her pleading as he walked slow-motion style to the bed, discarding his clothes with each airy step. "Leave us alone ... alone..." His voice echoed off into the distance. Samantha seemed to float weightlessly above the Christmas tree. When she hovered over the bed, Tony cast arctic eyes up to her. "Can't you see I'm still in love with her, Samantha?"

* * * * *

"Samantha. Samantha?" The voice now belonged to Adam. Perched on the side of the bed, he held her in his arms. She was awake now and shaking violently.

Dropping her head on his chest, she sobbed as if her heart were breaking. For a little while, Adam let her cry it out, then lifting her quivering chin with his fingers, he gazed into her red, swollen eyes. "You were having a nightmare, but it's over now."

"No!" she shook her head furiously. "It was real. It happened. She was in his bed mocking me. They were both mocking me!"

"That's enough!" he snapped. Then he laid her back gently on the pillows. "Close your eyes. I'll bring you some tea and aspirins. Once this fever breaks, you'll feel much better."

Minutes later, she was able to sleep again. Mercifully, it was a dreamless sleep. When she awoke just before noon, her forehead was cool and damp. The fever had broken.

"Welcome back," Adam said, wiping her brow tenderly with a towel. "You really had me worried there for a while."

Through bleary eyes, she looked at him. He was still unshaven and looked as if he had been ill himself. Weakly, she asked, "Have you been here all along?"

"Naturally," he drawled, assuming a cheerful tone. "I had to protect you like a criminal. What if the fever caused you to walk in your sleep and you wandered out into the hall. All my weird neighbors would have thought I was conducting some sort of strange orgy in here, and before long, I'd be fending them off with a whip and a chair."

Samantha couldn't help but laugh at the way he humorized everything. He had the magical gift of saying the right thing at the right time, and his unique method of cheering her up never failed to lift her downtrodden spirits. Tenderly, she touched the fine growth of hair on his face.

"I'd like to get up and take a shower," she said. "I feel so grubby."

Nodding his approval, he went to the side of the bureau where her luggage stood, opened it, and waited until Samantha pointed to her quilted robe and hair dryer. He brought them to her then left the room, looking more relaxed than he had all morning.

In the living room, a fire crackled in the red brick hearth. Bowls of hot soup and sandwiches were set for both of them on the coffee table. Still a little unsteady, she made her way to the sofa and curled up on it like a contented kitten. She had scrubbed her face until it glowed, and had brushed her thick hair into soft waves that circled her shoulders.

Adam was sitting on an ottoman waiting for her. Still in his robe, he apologized for his unkempt appearance. But Samantha couldn't have cared less. To her, he looked wonderful.

They had just finished their lunch and were relaxing over tea when a knock came at the door. Giving a loud groan, Adam ran his fingers quickly through his rumpled hair, tugged at the ties on his robe, and left to answer it. Samantha's heart fluttered in her throat when she heard Tony's velvety voice.

"May I come in, Pearce?" she heard him ask. "Well ... uh..." Adam sputtered uncomfortably. "Sure. Let me take your coat."

"You can take this, too," he said, pushing Samantha's purse into his hands. "She's been so busy running, I doubt she remembers where she left it."

Samantha's hands began to shake uncontrollably. She set her cup down onto the table, keeping her eyes fixed on the polished hardwood floor, afraid to look at him. She felt her heart drop as the cushions beside her gave with his weight.

After Adam hung Garrett's coat in the closet, he went to Samantha and asked if she would be okay. She wanted to say *no,* but a weak *yes* came out instead.

A blatant expression crossed Garrett's face as his eyes shifted back and forth from his wife to Adam, who were both in their nightwear.

Immediately, Adam surmised what Garrett was

thinking, but instead of trying to explain, he murmured faintly, "If you'll both excuse me, I think I'll go into the bathroom and slash my wrists."

"Don't go to any drastic measures on my account, Pearce," Garrett replied derisively.

Samantha lost her cool at his insolence. "Stop jumping to conclusions, Tony. Adam and I were–"

"Adam and you were *what*, Samantha?" he asked, a sardonic sneer curving his mouth.

Samantha's face flushed crimson. "Adam and I were only having lunch together, that's all."

"Really?" he drawled, crossing his arms over his chest. "In your bathrobes? How convenient. And does the menu include intimacy for desert?"

That did it! Blind fury raced through her, and without conscious thought, she brought her hand up and smashed her fingers hard across his face, her long nails barely missing his eyes. "How dare you insinuate that Adam and I are intimate!" she hissed vehemently.

His eyebrows rose mockingly. "You mean I'm mistaken? You two are innocent of any wrongdoing?"

"Absolutely." She refused to be intimidated. "Unlike you, I would never consider doing such a thing. I took a vow of fidelity, or have you forgotten?"

He gave her a cold smile. "Oh, I haven't forgotten. It's just that I was quick to assume that you had. After all, I'm human, just like you. And I can make errors in judgment, just like you."

She knew where he was leading her, and she was ready. "I made no error I judgment last night, Tony. Your lover spelled it out–"

"She's not my lover, damn it!" his voice cut in

scathingly.

"Of course not!" she returned with matched fury. "She's the Welcome Wagon Lady, and she made a special trip to your cabin on Christmas Day just to deliver her goodies!"

He shot to his feet and glared down at her. "Believe what you want. I'm through trying to get you to come to your senses."

"Is that why you came here?" she bellowed, "To bring me to my senses?"

"Not anymore!" he said roughly. "I came to tell you you've been booked as one of the guests on my show tomorrow night."

She pushed her hands into her wide sleeves. "I wasn't asked by your producer if I'm available tomorrow night, which I'm not. So, it must have been you who automatically booked me. Well, I hate to disappoint you, or worse yet, disrupt your schedule, but I won't be here. I'm going home to make arrangements for an annulment. Perhaps Rosemary can take my place on stage. Lord knows, she's taken my place in your bed."

To Garrett, that blatant remark was the last straw. With the agility of a cat, he reached down and swooped her up onto her feet. His eyes, narrowed and dangerous, were only inches away from hers. "You'll be on that show if I have to send armored guards to deliver you there. Do I make myself clear? You can pamper your bruised ego some other time. This concerns my job!"

"To hell with your job!" she spat viciously. "This concerns my life! And I want you out of it. The sooner, the better!"

He tightened his grip on her wrists. "I'm involved in

171

this marriage, too. What makes you think you can get out of it so easily?"

Contempt colored her tone. "It shouldn't be difficult. I'll charge you with adultery!"

"You have no grounds."

"The hell I don't! I was there, remember? I *saw* Rosemary in your bed without a stitch on."

"So what?" he argued. "You didn't see me in bed with her!"

"That doesn't mean anything," she said sarcastically. "You probably hopped in after I left."

He looked as if he had taken a kick in the chest. "You can't possibly believe that!"

Her gaze was direct. "She wouldn't have driven all the way to your cabin unless she was sure of getting what she came for."

"Prove it!" he demanded.

"I will."

"No you won't," he countered. "You can't. And that shoots the hell out of your adultery charge."

All this arguing was sapping Samantha of what little strength she had. Drained and bewildered, she slumped down on the sofa. Lowering her head into her hands, she sighed deeply. "What do I have to do to convince you I want out of this marriage?"

What she expected for an answer was anything other than what she got. He eased himself down beside her and took her face in his hands. A look of total defeat swept over his handsome features. "You really mean it, Samantha?" he breathed. "You really want me out of your life?"

"Yes," she choked miserably.

"Okay, I'll give you your freedom ... on one

condition."

"No!"

"Listen to me," he urged, his smoldering eyes caressing her angry face. "Make your appearance. Answer my questions about your book. I promise, no rough stuff. Do this for me, and you can have your annulment. Fair enough?"

Samantha gazed back at him. Right now, he looked so sad, so vulnerable, that she almost reached the point where it was becoming impossible to hold firm to her decision. Her heart couldn't deny the fact that she loved him. But, her head refused to be free of the image of Rosemary, and the undeniable fact that the woman was very much a part of his life, and had been, all along. Now was the moment that would decide the course of her life. What should she do? Follow her heart or her head?

Reason won out. "Fair enough."

CHAPTER TWELVE

Sitting stiffly on the plush sofa in the luxurious Plaza Hotel suite, Samantha checked her watch. Three hours to air time. She took a deep breath and tried to relax by repeating to herself that everything was going to turn out just fine. So, why was her heart banging away like a jackhammer? And why were her legs so wobbly?

The answer was simple. She didn't want to go on – didn't want to keep to her end of the bargain, and yet she knew she had no alternative. No show. No annulment.

The shrill of the telephone beside her made her jump. She picked up the receiver with a trembling hand.

"Samantha?"

"Yes, Tony," she responded, sighing. "What is it this time?" She hoped her feigned cool and indifferent attitude came through loud and clear.

"Just checking to see if you're pleased with your suite." Garrett knew her room was exquisite. He'd just wanted to hear her voice, hoping against hope that she was having second thoughts about leaving him. But the tone of her voice was expressionless, as though she were speaking to a stranger.

"It's fine," she stated bluntly.

"Good. I hope you don't think the hotel room was my idea. You could have refused and stayed with Pearce. It's just customary for our guests to stay at the Plaza. Makes them feel special. You know ... pampered." He was groping for words, anything, just to keep her on the line.

"I'm impressed," she said, dryly. "Is that all?" She

wanted to call a halt to this strained bit of prattle, fearing any moment her voice would crack and he would detect her acute anxiety. It would put him at an advantage, and she didn't want to give him the satisfaction of knowing she was practically a basket case.

"Not quite," he returned. "I thought you might be pleased to learn you won't be the only guest. Judge Ryan will also be there."

"Really?" Samantha replied in a surprised tone. Tonight of all nights. How convenient. I'm sure you had something to do with it."

"Naturally," he answered. "Can you think of a better time? Ryan opened up this can of worms, if you recall, which means he's vulnerable right now. I wasn't about to pass up this opportunity, so I had my staff put pressure on him to make an appearance. Simple as that."

Samantha knew there was much more to it, but she didn't want to hear it, nor did she want to stay on the line any longer. She was just about to say goodbye when Garrett spoke again. "After Ryan, there's a tennis player, and then you. You'll be the last guest. Nevertheless, you're expected to be there by eleven-thirty."

"I understand," she said, her lips quivering. "Thanks for calling and filling me in."

"Wait a minute!" he shouted brusquely before she had a chance to hang up. "I'd like to know if you've made your plane reservation."

She forced herself to keep her voice tightly controlled. "Yes, I have. My flight leaves at two thirty in the morning."

There was a slight pause and then, "is Pearce driving you to the airport?"

Her answer was swift. "No. He offered, but ... no. I'm

taking a taxi."

"Samantha..." His voice caressed her name. "Let me take you. Just give me this last chance to say goodbye privately. We haven't had a chance to–"

This was too much. "Tony ... please. Let's leave it as it is." She hung up the phone before he was able to utter another word. Bitter tears filled her eyes and she drew in a deep breath to hold back their escape.

* * * * *

"May I come in?" the familiar voice called out after tapping lightly on the door.

Samantha swallowed hard as she opened it. Adam stood there holding two coffees to go. Upon seeing him, her lips turned into a smile. "Well, Prince Charming, did you come to escort me to the ball?"

"Not this time, Cinderella," he said, and she noticed a muscle twitch nervously in his cheek. "I thought we might share a cup of coffee together before you leave for the studio."

She pointed to the sofa. "I'm glad you came, Adam. Thanks for the coffee."

"My, my," he drawled, sitting back deeper into the cushions, "aren't we tranquil tonight? No signs of stage fright, no last-minutes hysterics. Steady as a rock. I'm impressed. I truly am. Here I thought I'd find you biting your nails down to the quick, or crying your eyes out. Guess I got a lot to learn about women, especially the ones in love." He smiled wickedly at her, and just as he expected, she pounced on him. "What are you getting at? As if I didn't know."

The smile on his lips faded. "I'd hoped by now you'd smartened up and changed your mind about leaving Garrett."

She gave him a flinty glare. "Look," she snarled, and all her coolness vanished. "For the last time, stop hassling me about this. I know what I'm doing. I'm correcting a mistake that should never have happened."

"Your marriage happened because it was meant to," Adam said in a suddenly philosophical tone.

"The sinking of the Titanic should never have happened either, but it did," she growled. Why can't you accept it? I have."

"Oh, I've accepted the sinking of the big boat for a long time now," he retorted flippantly. It's this crazy talk about an annulment I find hard to swallow."

Her frustration at its peak, she took in a deep breath, then asked indignantly, "What is it to you, Adam? You're only an agent, not a marriage counselor. Why are you trying to get me to salvage a marriage that was wrong from the start?"

Adam looked puzzled. "You keep saying that. Why?"

"Because one minute the man wants my head on a platter, and the next, he's asking me to marry him – immediately, that very day! It was like he was beating the clock." She shook a pointed finger at him. "I'll bet my laptop he knew Rosemary was coming, and nothing you can say will convince me otherwise. Which means, he married me to get revenge against her. And why? Who knows, Adam? More importantly, who cares?"

"You do," he answered quickly. "But you're too stubborn to admit it and not woman enough to do something about it!"

"*That's enough!*" she snapped violently, and a rush of hot tears quickly filled her eyes. She turned her back to him, furious with herself for losing her self-control.

Adam knew he was getting nowhere, so he rose to his feet, turned her around, and took her chilled hands in his. "Okay, I give up," he conceded. "It's your life. You claim you know what you're doing. I don't happen to agree, but like you say, who am I to tell you you're making the biggest mistake of your life? I got a feeling, deep down in my gut, that you already know it. But your stubborn Irish pride..."

He stopped himself short and squeezed her hands tightly. "Good luck on the show. I'll be in touch in a couple of weeks."

As soon as he left, Samantha took a hot bath, which did little to relax her, then she began to dress. She had chosen to wear a black knit dress with a matching black and white jacket, choosing it because it was not only conservative enough for the show, but was comfortable for the plane ride home.

Home. The more she thought about Tampa, the more anxious she became. She kept asking herself why. Could it be she really didn't want to go home? Now she was being ridiculous. Or was she?

Her grooming completed, it was time to leave. Setting her luggage down beside the door, she checked the rooms once again to make sure she hadn't forgotten anything.

* * * * *

Due to the heavy traffic, Samantha didn't arrive at the studio until midnight. When she stepped off the elevator, she encountered an usher who took her to the Green Room.

When he opened the door, Samantha's gaze fell upon a casually dressed young woman who was seated on a brown leather sofa, her legs tucked under her. With her eyes fixed on a woman's magazine, she sipped a cup of coffee. She looked very familiar, but at the moment, Samantha couldn't place where she had seen her before. As the usher turned to leave, Samantha leaned close to him and whispered, "Who is she?"

"That's Pamela Holmes, the tennis champ," he whispered back. "She's on after Judge Ryan. Word's out that she's on the needle. If it's true, Garrett will get her to admit it. Then he'll nail her, and she can kiss her career goodbye. He's the best, or the worst, depending on how you look at it. But then, that's not news to you. You've already gone a round with him." He winked at Samantha. "Can't wait for round two. Should be some show." He turned to see if Pamela had heard him. She was still engrossed in her reading, so apparently, she did not. He closed the door behind him.

Samantha forced herself to ignore what the usher had said. Now was not the time to allow a smart-mouthed youth to antagonize her. She needed her energy for the interview.

Expelling her breath on a long sigh, she picked up her suitcase and gave a cursory look around the room. A long counter-like table stood directly opposite her. On one end was a large monitor for the waiting guests to view the activities taking place on stage. A coffee urn with Styrofoam cups and containers of milk and sugar sat on the opposite end. In the center was a bouquet of American Beauty roses with a card wedged among the greenery. Imagining they belonged to Miss Holmes, Samantha remarked offhandedly, "Lovely roses. From an admirer?"

Pamela Holmes gave Samantha a blatant look. "They're not for me. They're for some guy named Sam. And people think *I'm* weird." She lowered her eyes to the magazine and lost herself in her reading.

Immediately Adam came to mind, and Samantha chuckled. Who else but Adam would send her roses and address the card to 'Sam'? But when she read the card, her heart almost stopped when she read the brief message. *TO SAM. THE BUTLER DIDN'T DO IT, I DID. PLEASE FORGIVE ME. T.*

Naturally, anyone reading the card would have been baffled, but Samantha got its meaning. Momentarily she was so touched, she almost cried.

I have to be strong, she reminded herself. *He's only trying to chip away at my defenses.*

She slipped the card between the roses, then slid her luggage under the counter. After that, she poured herself a cup of coffee.

No sooner did she take a seat at the opposite end of the sofa when the show's producer opened the door and instructed Miss Holmes to follow him.

"Good luck," Samantha said as the girl checked her appearance in the full length mirror by the door.

"Yeah," she returned, sounding somewhat bored. "I hear he's out for my butt." She gave a quick chuckle, then left the room.

Alone now, Samantha felt her stomach tie up in knots, so she rested her head back against the sofa and began taking long, deep breaths. Calmness was just beginning to take hold when she remembered Garrett was interviewing Judge Ryan. She leaned forward and turned on the monitor. When the close-up shot of Garrett flashed on the screen, she turned up the volume. With moist eyes and an aching heart, she reached out and touched the screen, knowing it was the only way she would ever be able to touch his face again.

She watched intensely as the camera moved out to show both her husband and Judge Ryan. Garrett was bent forward in his seat clutching a rolled-up sheet of paper. Looking directly into the judge's eyes, he said, "I'm holding in my hands, a confirmed report that Lowell Townsmand, the current District Attorney for this state, is up for re-election next year. Am I right?"

"Of course," the judge answered calmly. "It's public knowledge."

"And, are contributions made to his campaign a matter of public record as well?" Garrett queried.

The judge's tone suddenly changed from calm to evasive. "That depends on who wants to know."

"The American taxpayer, for one," Garrett replied, somberly. "The Internal Revenue Service for another. And–"

"What's your point, Garrett?" the judge cut in, shifting nervously in his seat as though he knew what his host was leading up to. And he was right.

Garrett slowly unfolded the sheet of paper and looked down at it. "Do you always contribute one hundred thousand dollars to ensure your candidate's successful election?"

"No," the judge answered, practically whispering.

"I didn't think so," Garrett retorted. "But you did this time, didn't you? *And* you used the taxpayer's money, not your own." He pointed to a section in the paper. "It says so, right here. Why didn't you use your own dough?"

The judge lowered his eyes, embarrassed. "I didn't want Mrs. Ryan to know."

The audience gave a slight chuckle, but Garrett was dead somber. "My sympathy goes out to your wife, Ryan. She's a lovely woman who thinks you're a saint. Well, I'm sure she's watching this broadcast, probably crying her eyes out over this damning revelation. Unfortunately, there's more..."

"Don't go there, Garrett!" the judge bellowed, sweating profusely, "not if you value your life!"

Garrett wasn't moved by the man's threat. "It's not my life that's at stake here, *your honor*. It's your freedom, which ends tonight!"

The judge bolted to his feet, his face soaked with perspiration. "What the hell are you talking about?"

Garrett held his anger in check. "Give it up, Ryan. That healthy contribution you made didn't go towards Townsmand's campaign, it went to fund his drug habit. It's all right here in this report." He tossed the paper onto the table beside him. "Townsmand and the police are waiting for you downstairs. Security will escort you out."

"You no good son-of-a-bitch," Ryan bellowed, as Garrett turned to the camera and announced it was time for a commercial break.

* * * * *

When the camera lights blinked on again, Garrett was studying the notes on his next guest. It seemed the more he read, the deeper the lines became embedded around his mouth. The tension emitted by him was brutally apparent.

Samantha's heart went out to Pamela Holmes. If her husband could crucify a judge on national television, she knew the young tennis star didn't stand a chance. And she was right. For the next twenty minutes, Garrett put the personal and professional life of the young woman through a sieve. Never allowing an evasive answer to elude him, he persisted with his third degree manner of interrogation until in a fit of utter defeat, Pamela Holmes admitted to the charges to which she was being accused.

As usual, the audience was right with Garrett – cheering and applauding him each time he fired damaging and degrading questions at her. When her allotted time was over, the young woman ran from the studio in tears, her career in dire jeopardy.

By this time, Samantha was feeling physically ill. In Garrett's present state of mind, she feared the worst for herself. If he dared to be so ruthless to a State Supreme Court judge and a celebrated sports figure, he was certain to put her through the proverbial wringer. It didn't matter that he had promised not to; she was still afraid. After all, he had a personal vendetta against her.

Before she knew it, Louie Polcheck stood in the doorway waving her on. She followed on unsteady legs as he led her backstage to her place behind the green satin curtain. Although she tried to will away all negative thoughts, she could not. Her troubled mind was centered on one thing and one thing only. Would he dare blurt their marriage to the nation? He had promised not to. They were going their separate ways. Therefore he wouldn't dare, she told herself. For doing so would cause a scandal – a situation he admitted wanting to avoid like the plague. She remembered his telling her he couldn't afford unfavorable publicity. Yet somehow, she didn't trust him.

* * * * *

Samantha held her breath as she watched all three cameras roll in for a close-up of Garrett. His back was to her, but she could still see him drop his note pad on the glass coffee table beside him. The red light on one of the cameras blinked on, and Garrett rose to his full height. Looking away from the cameras, he spoke directly to his audience.

"A couple of weeks ago, I made some very uncomplimentary remarks about a mystery writer who was about to join me on stage. I said some pretty derogatory things about him and his craft without giving the writer a chance to prove his credibility. And, of course, you all know what happened. The author turned out to be a lady ... a very lovely, aggressive young lady."

The audience began to howl, and Garrett, expecting the outburst, waited for them to stop.

"Since that time, the phones here at the studio have been ringing off the hooks. So we've invited the young lady back. And now it gives me great pleasure to introduce Sam McCall."

He turned in the direction of the curtain and began applauding along with the audience, who upon hearing her name, rose from their seats to greet her with a standing ovation. Somehow her legs managed to move her forward, and she found herself standing on center stage with him. Deafening whistles and cheers accompanied their hearty applause that seemed to go on forever. A huge wave of stage fright swept over her, causing her heart to pound in her ears, and her vision became blurred and distorted.

Garrett, taking in the pallor of her face, sensed her terror and quickly led her to one of the leather seats behind them.

She sat down, grateful to be off unsteady legs. As he clipped a tiny microphone on the lapel of her jacket, he gave her a dispassionate look, then took his seat beside her.

The audience stopped their cheering and, within seconds, an eerie quiet permeated the studio. Without wasting a moment, the cameras moved within inches of their faces. Samantha curled her fingers into her palms, wondering how she was ever going to live through this ordeal. Right now, it seemed a fate worse than death.

Leaning his elbows on the arms of his chair, he crossed his fingers over his lips. "If I promise to behave myself, do I have your word you'll spare me a repeat performance of the last time you were here?" he asked, giving a conspiratorial wink to the audience. If he had looked at her when he uttered that superfluous comment, she might have blurted out a weak, timid response. But she realized he was playing up to his viewers, performing for them, and the realization fired her with animosity. The terror vanished, and her senses returned. She flashed piercing green eyes upon him and replied in a voice that was clear and controlled, "Absolutely, providing you don't put your foot in your mouth again."

The audience chuckled, and Garrett, momentarily taken aback, shifted uncomfortably in his seat. "Touché," he said. "It was the one and only time I admit to making a mistake."

Samantha arched a fine brow and retorted quickly, "Wrong again, Mr. Garrett. I know of another time. But we're here to discuss my book, so shall we get on with it?"

Garrett seemed to know instinctively a war was being staged, and to Samantha's dismay, he was ready for it. He

185

bent forward, and resting his forearms on his powerful thighs, remarked flippantly, "I'm ready any time you are. Now, why don't you tell us why you write under the name, Sam."

Samantha looked into the depths of his eyes. "To sell my books. Why else?" she asked, feeling a bit smug. "As a writer of macabre mysteries, I figured it was more advantageous to use a man's pseudonym."

"I see," he said, nodding, and she saw his blue eyes darken. "So your intent was to deceive the public into believing you were a man."

The way he verbalized it made Samantha blush. "Well ... uh ... yes and no," she sputtered, wondering why he was making her feel like an idiot for writing under an alias. Defensively, she tried to explain. "Most writers prefer *not* to use their given name. My genre practically demands it."

"What is your given name?" he fired, ignoring her explanation.

It didn't dawn on her what he was leading up to, and she swallowed hard, feeling now like a criminal on trial. "Samantha Rose McCall," she rasped, breathing anxiously.

Picking up the notes from the coffee table, he pretended to devour them carefully. When he was through, he tossed them back on the table. "That's strange," he drawled, in that deep velvety voice, "my notes state your legal name to be Samantha Rose McCall *Garrett*."

Samantha felt her heart jump and she blushed crimson. He wouldn't dare! But he did. He reached over and gently caressed the gold band on her fourth finger. "Is this a wedding ring?" he asked, smiling a little crookedly.

He knew darn well it was. He was intimidating her and she was beginning to hate him for it. Narrowing her

186

eyes, she muttered through clenched teeth, "You might say that."

He turned his face to the side and touched the tip of his ear. "Would you kindly repeat that? I don't think the audience heard you."

"Really, Mr. Garrett!" she hissed, leaning forward in her seat. "I–"

"Just answer the question," he ordered.

It was no use. He was bound and determined to get her to admit she was married to him. Realizing there was no way around it, and suddenly wanting to get it over with, she snapped bitterly, "Yes."

Satisfied, he turned to the camera and said in a taunting voice, "Time for a station break, folks. We'll return in three minutes."

The red light blinked off, and a string of commercials flashed simultaneously on the monitors above the stage. Garrett turned his back on her as if she weren't there. He was being rude and impossible. She was about to let go with a string of don't-you-dares, when Louie Polcheck appeared from behind the curtain. Looking flustered as usual, he spoke sharply to Garrett. "You've only got about five minutes to wrap this up. Forget about this guy she's married to and get back to the beefy stuff!" He turned to leave, calling out to a stage hand as he disappeared behind the curtain.

Samantha couldn't believe what she had heard. Apparently Louie Polcheck wasn't paying attention, or he would've never ordered his host to change the subject. Garrett had gotten to the *beefy* stuff, and the audience had picked up on it. It was evident by their murmurings and muffled laughter.

Livid with rage, she pushed her face close to his. "How could you?" she hissed. "You promised me. *You promised me!*"

Tossing his head back, Garrett laughed. "So I did. But now I have a show to wrap up, and I'm going to leave this audience with what they came for – excitement, thrills, and a climax to end all climaxes."

Samantha became indignant. "Go ahead. But I'll get my revenge. I'll go to the press and announce the annulment. That will put you on the front page of all the gossip tabloids. To hell with your precious reputation!"

"And your picture will be right there with mine, sweetheart." He paused and grinned. "Now how will that sit with your folks?"

Samantha was so angry, she jumped up and was ready to stalk off the stage when Garrett quickly caught her by the wrist and pulled her down. "Stay right where you are!" he growled. "Don't you dare pull a trick like that on me again!"

There was no time to argue with him. The camera man was giving Garrett his cue. In a minute they'd be back on the air.

"Please," she begged, appealing to whatever shred of decency he might still possess, "if you don't care about making me look like a fool, at least consider my folks. Don't embarrass them just to satisfy your audience. You might be without dignity, but they're not. Please, I beg of you."

He looked at her and, after contemplating for a moment, replied calmly, "I'll drop it if you'll drop the annulment."

Reason left her altogether. "No!"

"Then get ready for the fireworks."

188

The red light blinked on and, before she knew it, Garrett grabbed her hand and began leading her towards the audience. With inner rage burning her cheeks, she could do nothing but walk stiffly beside him. When he reached the edge of the stage, he stopped. From the corner of her eye, she could see a muscle twitch spasmodically in his cheek. The moment she had dreaded had come.

"Ladies and gentlemen," he began, and Samantha felt the blood in her veins turn to ice. "I'm sure you've guessed by now that Miss McCall is, in reality, Mrs. Tony Garrett."

As if a bomb had exploded under them, the audience jumped quickly to their feet, each member howling and clapping with such enthusiasm, it brought tears to Samantha's eyes. That he could do this to her in front of millions of people after he had given his word proved he was not only ruthless, he was insufferable. If it were the last thing she would ever do, she would rake him through the mud for humiliating her like this.

When the audience finally quieted down and settled back into their seats, Garrett, glorying in the ovation, announced that the lady by his side had become his wife on Christmas Day, and for the next two weeks they would be taking an extended honeymoon. Pulling her possessively to him, he waved to the audience and bade them goodnight.

* * * * *

The camera light blinked off, and Louie Polcheck dashed out from behind the curtain. Chomping on his unlit cigar, the frazzled producer marched over to Garrett. In a burst of outrage, he proceeded to reprimand his exuberant host. "What the hell do you think you're doing?" he

189

bellowed, yanking the cigar from between his clenched teeth. "You can't take any more time off! You have a–"

"Simmer down, Louie," Garrett scolded as he released his hold on Samantha to put both hands on the shoulders of the irascible old man.

Samantha took the opportunity and made her escape. Seething with resentment, she scurried off the stage and ran into the Green Room, slamming the door behind her. She leaned against it, her heart pounding savagely. "How dare he!" she sputtered, her breath coming in rapid spurts. For sure now, she wanted nothing more than to be rid of him forever, and spent a lot more energy trying to convince herself of that fact.

Somewhere in the midst of her tirade, she heard the mingling voices of the production crew showering their congratulations on Garrett out in the hall. Realizing there would be no chance to get away undetected, she gritted her teeth and yanked her jacket from the coat rack beside the sofa. She was still fuming when the door flew open and Garrett barged into the room. Whirling on her heels, she shot him a hateful look, expecting to encounter the smile of victory stamped on his face. But the lines around his mouth were deep, and his eyes were hard and cold as they met hers.

Without a word, he picked up her suitcase, then grabbed her by the arm and pulled her towards the door. Fighting him off, Samantha spat out, "Put down my suitcase and release me before I call the security guards and have you arrested for kidnapping!"

"Kidnapping!" he sneered. "Lady, if I had the time, I'd put you across my knee and spank the daylights out of you for behaving like a spoiled child! But you have a plane to catch, and I'm going to make sure you're on it. Now, keep your mouth shut and come with me!"

When she saw that he was leading her away from the elevators, she flared automatically. "Where are you taking me? This isn't the way out of the building!"

"We're going to my dressing room," he growled. "Do you mind if I get my coat?"

"Yes I mind," she hissed. "I mind everything you do. I mind the way you push me around like a rag doll. And I mind the way you–"

Stopping abruptly, he dropped her suitcase on the floor and crushed her trembling body hard against his. Their lips barely touching, he drawled, "Did you mind the way I touched you in bed, Samantha? Did you mind the way our bodies rocked together until you couldn't stand it any longer and you begged me to make love to you?"

Samantha was so taken aback by his words and his nearness there in front of the production staff, that she couldn't utter a word.

"No, you didn't mind," he continued, "but you're going to mind being away from me and, most of all, you're going to mind not going on the romantic honeymoon I had planned for us. Now, hurry up and get inside," he growled, opening his dressing room door, "or you'll miss your plane!"

Once inside the dimly lit room, Samantha gasped. There, seated on Tony's black leather couch, was Rosemary.

"Take a seat," he ordered.

"I prefer to stand!" she spat, fed up with doing his bidding.

"You'll sit!" he barked, "or you can forget about getting to the airport on time!"

191

His vicious tone was like a slap in the face. Dulled, senseless with shock, Samantha sat down next to the woman.

"All right," he said, his voice more controlled as he slumped into his seat at the dressing table. "Before we part company, I want this matter of Rosemary and me cleared up." He looked at the woman and snapped briskly, "Tell her and make it brief!"

As usual, Samantha couldn't remain silent. With green eyes wide as a doe's caught in a pair of headlights, she gripped the arm of the couch and laughed haughtily. "Whatever you have to say, Rosemary, I don't want to hear it."

Rosemary casually toyed with her blonde waves. Looking somewhat bored and uncaring, she said, "I'm sure you don't, darling, but Tony dragged me down here for this little tête-à-tête, so—"

Samantha regarded Rosemary with exasperation. "I don't have time to listen to what you have to say. You've already told me you two were lovers, so it's not necessary."

"Oh, we were more than lovers, darling," Rosemary admitted quickly, "we were husband and wife. That is, until Tony caught me in bed with another man – a good friend of his who just happened to be married to somebody else. The problem was that he wouldn't leave his wife to marry me. He just wanted to have an affair. Well, I wasn't about to be the *other* woman in his life, so I got even with him and married Tony. Then there was the issue with Tony's best friend, Charlie. But that's another story.

"I had hoped that Tony still loved me. So, I continued to pursue him. But, he never gave in – and I never gave up. My last ditch effort was when I paid a stagehand here at the studio to tell me where I could find Tony. He said that Tony was up at Hunter Mountain for Christmas. Of course, I didn't know about you."

She squared her shoulders and went on. "Anyway, that night after you ran away, Tony told me that he was head over heels in love with you, and that you both had just gotten married. He also said that there would never be a chance for us again."

She turned to Garrett, looking regretful. "He's a catch, darling, a real catch. Too bad you're leaving him. Someday you'll kick yourself for doing this. I know. I've been kicking myself ever since I cheated on him."

She got up from the couch and rested her hand on Samantha's arm. "Tony wasn't unfaithful to you," she said, remorsefully, then quickly left the room.

Feeling shamed to the bone for not trusting him, Samantha looked forlornly at Garrett's reflection in the mirror. His face held no emotion. He seemed detached, as though lost in his own thoughts. Rising to her feet, she made her way slowly and unsteadily to him. When she reached his side, she turned and perched herself on the edge of the dressing table. Her heart was pounding so loudly she was sure he could hear it.

Just as she was about to speak, Garrett snarled, "If you're going to apologize, forget it. It's too late for that now."

His conceited attitude shook her. "Don't flatter yourself," she said coldly. "You staged that little confession for your own benefit as well as mine. But you should have saved yourself the trouble. It accomplished nothing. Furthermore, if anyone deserves an apology, it's–"

Without a warning, he pulled her to him and planted

his mouth on hers, hard at first, then gently. Shocked by his impetuousness, she was momentarily confused. When she finally realized what was happening, she raised one hand to ward him off. Then, changing her mind, she dropped it listlessly to her side. His lips were so warm and soft, the feel of them spun her round and round in a series of mindless whirls, and for the moment she was without coherent thought.

He kissed her until she gasped for breath, then with one throaty groan, he pushed her away. "There," he uttered sarcastically, "you got your apology. Satisfied?"

"No, I'm not satisfied!" she retorted, feeling mocked and degraded. "Did you think that all you had to do was kiss me and the slate would be wiped clean? What I did to you in no way compares to what you subjected me to tonight. And, if you were half a man, you'd get down on your knees and beg my forgiveness" She was so angry that a rush of tears sprang to her eyes.

"Don't you dare cry!" he barked.

"Stop giving me orders!" she returned bitterly. "I'm not one of your staff, I'm your wife, damn it! Why didn't you stick to your word so we could have parted like civilized people!"

For a brief moment, Garrett's voice softened. "Look, Samantha. I didn't mean to be malicious. Believe–"

"The hell you didn't!" she broke in rapidly. "Getting even with me for leaving you became your personal crusade. Well, I'm sorry I did it. Okay? I was wrong. I made a stupid mistake and I'm sorry for everything."

"I'm sure you are," he answered dryly, "now that you know the truth. I can see by your display of remorse that it was quite a revelation to you. But all this has been an eye opener for me, too. You see, even though you're thirty-one, you're still a kid. You proved it by running away. You didn't trust me. Had you stayed and listened to me, all this could have been avoided, and we would have been spared this moment. As much as I hate to admit it, Rosemary has what it takes. She may be fickle, but she's got guts. She fights till the end for what she wants."

He stopped and ran agitated fingers through his hair. "I demand complete trust *in* and *from* my wife. My job involves me with women all the time. I can't be worrying that she's going to resort to jealous rages every time she sees me in what may appear to be a threatening situation. I don't need that kind of aggravation. That's why I waited so long to get married again. I thought I'd found the woman I could trust ... a woman who trusted me. I see I was wrong."

Samantha's insides went cold with dread. "You weren't wrong, Tony," she said, her voice crackling. "I'm still the girl you–"

"That's just it," he broke in. "You're still a girl. I'm a man, and I want a woman." He picked up the suitcase. "Let's go. We'll have to hurry as it is."

* * * * *

Samantha's gaze followed Garrett as he took long strides down the hall. The studio was quiet. When a man appeared from the shadows and approached, she heard Garrett give an order to have a taxi brought around to the front of the building. Then both men headed in the direction of the elevators.

Once they were out of sight, Samantha gave in to the anguish she was not allowed to release in his presence. She let the tears flow freely down her cheeks and watched as they dropped down onto the dressing table. The mess she had made of things was tearing her apart. Garrett didn't want her. He wanted a *woman*. By running away, she had behaved like an adolescent. She didn't deserve him, and now she was going to lose him forever.

Her red, swollen eyes lifted to the mirror. Suddenly, Adam's solemn face seemed to take form. It peered back at her angrily. *"I told you you were making the biggest mistake of your life. Now he's gone ... gone ... gone..."*

"Stop it! She cried, pressing her palms tightly against her temples. She blinked her eyes rapidly, and the image vanished. After she grabbed a handful of tissues from a box on the table, she dabbed at her eyes angrily, then half-ran from the room. By the time she reached the double glass doors that led to the street, Garrett was waiting in the taxi. When he saw her approach, he leaned over and pushed open the door. She had barely enough time to settle in before the cab swung into the heavy stream of traffic.

"Will we make it in time?" she asked anxiously, hoping against hope that the confrontation with Rosemary had used up all the allotted time.

Garrett checked his watch. "Yes."

He returned his stare to the road ahead, and Samantha knew if she stopped talking, he would maintain his silent attitude for the duration of the trip. Unfortunately, it was impossible to make small talk. Despair filled her heart. She didn't want to let him go, and yet, she couldn't find the right words to make him change his mind. Then it came to her.

Brazenly, she slid a bit closer and placed her hand lightly on his arm. "Tony," she breathed, "why don't you come with me to Florida? We could take that honeymoon and–"

"Sorry," he blurted, keeping his eyes on the road. "Nice try though. I told you you'd be wanting to take that honeymoon with me. But honeymoons are for happily married people. We're getting an annulment, remember?"

His tone of voice was so insulting, so icy, it infuriated her. In a voice as cold as his, she retorted, "You're absolutely right. We are getting an annulment. And you know something? I'm glad. I wouldn't stay married to you if you were the last man on the planet! You're a deceitful, conniving boar!"

"Keep your voice down," he snarled under his breath. Her lips curled contemptuously.

"Don't tell me what to do!" And then it all came out of Samantha with a fury she could no longer contain. "I can't believe I was stupid enough to try to change your mind! I must have been temporarily insane, because you're not worthy of my love – or anyone else's for that matter. You think you're so righteous sitting up there on your leather throne waiting to execute anyone who crosses you. Well, you got all your shots in tonight. You accomplished all you set out to do. I'm sure you're quite pleased with yourself."

"Is it okay to stop now, Mr. Garrett?" the taxi driver asked, bringing the cab to a halt before a high rise building.

"Yes, driver," Garrett answered, and before Samantha had a chance to voice her objection, Garrett opened the door and stepped out of the cab. After paying the driver, he instructed the man to remove Samantha's suitcase from the trunk.

The driver complied, and Samantha could tell from the look of relief on his face that he was glad to be rid of them, or at least, her. To be sure, he had heard her lash out profusely at the famous host, so when Garrett bade him goodnight, the driver eyed him sympathetically.

Samantha couldn't have cared less that she had caused a scene. She was even more furious now to discover she had not been taken to the airport. Leering at Garrett, she clenched her fists. "I demand to know what's going on!"

"Put a lid on it!" he flared. "Just come with me."

Samantha stared at him disbelievingly. She should have known he had another trick up his sleeve. Wasn't his cold rejection enough? Now he had purposely caused her to miss her plane. It was the last straw. "No!" she growled. "I don't know what you're up to this time, and I don't want to know. Just hand me my suitcase. I'll get my own taxi."

The sidewalk was crowded even for this time of night. But Garrett disregarded the incredulous stares and snickers of the passers-by. With one quick move he grabbed her by the upper arm and pulled her along with him.

To protest would've accomplished nothing, Samantha decided, so she silenced her rage and followed him into the building.

Upon entering the elegant lobby, he marched her straight to the elevator. Fortunately for her the elevator was empty, so no one saw him give her a shove on her backside to advance her forward. Once inside, he pressed the button marked Penthouse. Seconds later, the doors parted. Garrett motioned her out, but Samantha refused to budge.

"Come," he whispered gently as he extended his hand. Suddenly, all the fight went out of her. She moved as if in a trance, following closely behind as he led her down the hall, stopping before a polished cherry wood door. After inserting a key in the lock, he swung the door open, then touched a button on the wall to the right. Immediately, the room became bathed in a warm, soft light. Putting his hand at her waist, Garrett led her inside, then stepped back into the hall for her luggage.

"Let me guess," she said softly, keeping her eyes fixed on him as he placed the bag alongside the wall. "This is your apartment." As he closed the door, she turned, giving the room a hasty appraisal. It was gorgeous.

"Not exactly," he said, offhandedly. "It's yours."

"Mine?" Perplexed, she frowned and looked back at him.

"That's right, *Mrs.* Garrett." He smiled. "It's my wedding present to you."

Samantha was so stunned, so confused, she burst into tears.

"Now what's wrong?" he asked, his thick brows knitting together.

"Oh, Tony!" This was just too much to take. After a night of continuing emotional trauma, her composure crumbled around her. "None of this makes any sense. I can't figure you out, and what's more, I'm too tired to try. I only know I want to go home."

"You are home, sweetheart," he muttered huskily. "Now, give me your jacket."

"Please don't," she begged, exhausted. "No more of your schemes."

"This is no scheme, Samantha, this is truly your home – our home. I brought you here so that we could be completely alone. We need to talk calmly and rationally about our marriage ... about us. Then, if you still want to go, I won't stop you." He took their coats and tossed them onto a nearby chair.

Placing his arm around her waist, he guided her to a

massive gold velvet sectional sofa that dominated the room. It was the largest couch Samantha had ever seen. It was so soft it felt like a cloud beneath her tense, tired body. Sighing deeply, she leaned her head back on the cushions and closed her eyes.

She felt the cushions give with Garrett's weight. The heady male smell of him made her senses reel. Keeping her eyes closed, she told herself she should leave immediately. But she couldn't move.

"Comfortable?" he asked, stretching his long muscular body dangerously close to hers.

"Mmmmm," she purred, feeling all the tension drain out of her. "Who wouldn't be? This is absolute heaven, absolute–"

Before she could finish, Garrett took her in his arms and pressed her tightly against him. He lowered his lips to the hollow of her throat, spilling thrills of pleasure along her sensitive skin. A wildfire raced through her as his lips banished all her defenses. This was madness, to be sure, but she was powerless against him. It was when he traced her lower lip ever so lightly with his that she caught herself and jerked her head away, saying, "I don't understand, and I can't forget the way you treated me so coldly in your dressing room. You were so anxious to get rid of me. Now you bring me here to talk? Well, talk."

"I love you and want you," he moaned against her ear. "Tell me you love and want me, too. I can't stand this fighting between us anymore."

She responded not with words, but by sliding his suit jacket off his massive frame. Smiling, he released his hold on her and let the jacket fall to the thick, plush carpeting. Then, with fingers that seemed to have a mind of their own, she undid his tie and shirt.

When his shirt and tie joined his jacket on the rug, he bent down over Samantha and looked soulfully into her eyes. "I mean to have you," he said, his heavy veiled look tantalizing her. "You realize there's no turning back for me now."

Samantha's only response was a low, throaty moan. When she reached up to caress his face, he turned his lips into the palm of her hand. Ablaze with passion, he reached down and removed her soft jacket. The rest of her clothing soon followed. Samantha gave a slight shiver, and Garrett lowered himself down gently. She began to moan as she pressed her soft breasts into the thick mat of hair covering his chest.

The soft, velvet cushions enveloped them like a glove, its warmth transforming her shivers into an explosion of passion.

Garrett was lost in the feel of her. His strong hand traveled down slowly to caress her full, round breast.

His touch had a dizzying effect on her and she was unable to contain her desire. "Oh, God, Tony ... please..." she begged, writhing under the hand at her breast.

But Garrett wasn't ready to put an end to Samantha's yearning. A smile played on his lips, and unhurriedly he kissed her parted lips, leaving her begging for more. Their bodies fused hungrily together and Garrett luxuriated in the moment as he grasped her hips tightly to him, moaning tenderly while his tongue explored the deep recesses of her mouth. "Sweetheart ... oh, my beautiful wife. Let me love you now and for the rest of our lives."

Time hung suspended as they clung to each other, both now out of control as their passions mounted, then erupted in a series of wild, violent explosions.

Thoroughly exhausted, Garrett rested his head on his wife's breasts and sighed deeply. "I suppose an apology is in order, but the truth is, I'm not sorry one bit."

She sank her lips into his dark, wavy hair. "You planned this right from the beginning, didn't you?"

He rolled away and, turning on his back, gazed stonily at the ceiling. "I had to or I would have lost you forever."

She rose up on her elbow and looked at him. "But that's what you wanted, remember?"

"No. That's what *you* wanted," he said. "Consider the night you ran away. Did you think it was easy for me to go to the Ryan's to get you to come back? You're my wife. Even if you felt betrayed, which you did, you could have at least let me explain. But no. Right away you wanted an annulment."

"It was our wedding night, Tony, and another woman was in your bed." Samantha couldn't hide the anguish in her voice. "She claimed you two were lovers and–"

"And I told you she was lying. Why didn't you believe me? Trust me? If I had wanted her, I never would have married you, would I?"

When Samantha didn't answer, he went on. "I will admit I had a hunch Rosemary had learned where I was and might come to the cabin. That's why I pressured you to marry me right away. I figured once she saw that we were legally married, she'd finally give up and leave. I never dreamed she'd be brazen enough to take off her clothes and hop into bed. But then again, I never figured you'd be hiding in the Christmas tree, either."

The reminder of that classic blunder brought a roar of laughter from both of them.

"You should have seen the look on your face when the tree and I came crashing down before you." Samantha giggled.

"You should've seen the look on yours," Garrett retorted, chuckling. "Talk about getting caught with your hand in the cookie jar. You looked so guilty ... but so adorable."

Samantha's face went scarlet. "Nobody's adorable covered with pine needles and tinsel. I was a fright and felt like an idiot. But at the time, running away seemed my only option. Seems like I've been running away from you since the beginning."

Garrett raised an eyebrow at her. "Now that this mess has been cleared up, don't you think it's time we stopped fighting?"

Samantha looked at her husband and was slow to answer. "I might have been wrong about a lot of things, but I'm not wrong when I say you're still the most conniving, deceitful man I've ever met. And it's going to be a long time before I forgive you for breaking your promise to me."

"I was angry and hurt," he said, pulling her back into his arms. "I wanted to hurt you back. No woman has ever gotten under my skin the way you have. I couldn't be rational about anything. All I know is that I wanted you from the beginning. I didn't need a long, drawn-out courting period to sort out my feelings. What difference did it make if we got married right away? I would've insisted on it even if Rosemary wasn't in the picture. But after you left, I went into a rage. I wanted revenge. So, I set it up with my producer to get you back on the show, and to ensure it, I agreed to the annulment. But, believe me, no matter what transpired in my dressing room, I wasn't going to let you leave me. I may be all those terrible things you said, and you have every right to hate me, but the heart of the matter is that I love you."

His mouth moved hungrily over hers. Then she drew back and looked him in the eyes. "Was I woman enough for you a short while ago?"

"Sweetheart, you're more than enough woman for me. Now stop this silly chatter and let's get on with our honeymoon."

~Excerpt, Available Now~

Unforgettable

Robert regretted giving Maddie that last drink. Giggling, she raised her hand and pointed a manicured fingernail at him. "Do you know you have the same name as the famous writer who writes those silly plays? His name is Robert Kendall, too. Why, you even *look* like him!" She gave her thigh a slap. "Hot damn! I'll bet people ask for your autograph, thinking you're him. And you sign 'em too, don'tcha, you sly little devil."

Robert gave a low laugh. She was just too cute to resist. Playing along with her, he drawled, "Yup. I sign every one. That's because I really am him."

"No!" She giggled again.

Robert shook his head and smiled. "It's true. I am. I have no reason to lie."

"All men lie," she remarked dryly, her mind flashing back to that afternoon and Alex.

Robert picked up on it. "My guess is that you've been burned, and badly. Who hasn't? But don't judge me by someone else." He rose from his seat and turned the radio on.

The haunting rendition of *Unforgettable* enveloped the room. The soul-wrenching duet by the late Nat King Cole and his daughter had been Alex's love song to her. Now he was gone, and the melody cut through Maddie like a knife.

~Excerpt, Coming Soon~

Dark Crescendo

Carlton Reed lunged at Nick Jordan. Grabbing him by the shirt collar, he pulled him forward and bellowed, "What kind of a man seduces a woman two weeks after her husband's death? And in a public restaurant, yet!"

"It wasn't like that at all, Father," Joanna broke in. "Nick didn't force himself on me. I went to him willingly. In fact, Nick came here to ask me to marry him, and I have accepted."

"Have you taken leave of your senses, child?" Carlton asked disbelievingly.

"For the love of God, Father, will you stop regarding me as a child? I am an adult, and I thought I'd made that point abundantly clear to you last night, or have you seen fit–"

"I haven't forgotten last night," he snapped back. "But I sure in hell didn't interpret your bid for freedom as a license to behave like a common trollop, especially with the likes of a Nick Jordan! This time you've scraped the bottom of the barrel, Joanna, and it shames me to discover the depths to which you will sink, all in the name of love!"

~About the Author~

LUCILLE NAROIAN

 A resident of northern Massachusetts and the mother of a grown son, Lucille Naroian has held a variety of jobs, including cosmetologist, chiropractor's assistant, pharmacy technician, and administrator in the stock market. In addition to indulging her love of writing, Lucille is an award-winning portrait artist and enjoys tending her aquarium of tropical fish.

Lucille's second published romance novel, **Unforgettable**, is available now, with **Dark Crescendo** coming soon. Look for Lucille's books at Amazon and other popular book retailers.

To learn more about Lucille and her books, please visit her web site at...

www.LucilleNaroian.com

Lucille enjoys hearing from readers and can be contacted by visiting Penumbra Publishing's web site at...

www.PenumbraPublishing.com

CPSIA information can be obtained at www.ICGtesting.com
Printed in the USA
BVOW05s1033230215

388900BV00001B/25/P